Back by Popular Demand

A collector's edition of favorite titles
from one of the world's best-loved
romance authors. Harlequin is proud to
bring back these sought after titles and
present them as one cherished collection.

BETTY NEELS:
COLLECTOR'S EDITION

A GEM OF A GIRL
WISH WITH THE CANDLES
COBWEB MORNING
HENRIETTA'S OWN CASTLE
CASSANDRA BY CHANCE
VICTORY FOR VICTORIA
SISTER PETERS IN AMSTERDAM
THE MAGIC OF LIVING
SATURDAY'S CHILD
FATE IS REMARKABLE
A STAR LOOKS DOWN
HEAVEN IS GENTLE

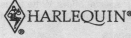

HARLEQUIN®

Betty Neels spent her childhood and youth in Devonshire before training as a nurse and midwife. She was an army nursing sister during the war, married a Dutchman, and subsequently lived in Holland for fourteen years. She now lives with her husband in Dorset, and has a daughter and grandson. Her hobbies are reading, animals, old buildings and, of course, writing. Betty started to write on retirement from nursing, incited by a lady in a library bemoaning the lack of romantic novels.

Mrs. Neels is always delighted to receive fan letters, but would truly appreciate it if they could be directed to Harlequin Mills & Boon Ltd., 18-24 Paradise Road, Richmond, Surrey, TW9 1SR, England.

Books by Betty Neels

HARLEQUIN ROMANCE

Don't miss any of our special offers. Write to us at the following address for information on our newest releases.

Harlequin Reader Service
U.S.: 3010 Walden Ave., P.O. Box 1325, Buffalo, NY 14269
Canadian: P.O. Box 609, Fort Erie, Ont. L2A 5X3

BETTY NEELS

HENRIETTA'S OWN CASTLE

COLLECTOR'S EDITION

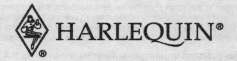

HARLEQUIN®

TORONTO • NEW YORK • LONDON
AMSTERDAM • PARIS • SYDNEY • HAMBURG
STOCKHOLM • ATHENS • TOKYO • MILAN • MADRID
PRAGUE • WARSAW • BUDAPEST • AUCKLAND

ISBN 0-373-83389-X

HENRIETTA'S OWN CASTLE

First North American Publication 1976.

Copyright © 1975 by Betty Neels.

All rights reserved. Except for use in any review, the reproduction or
utilization of this work in whole or in part in any form by any electronic,
mechanical or other means, now known or hereafter invented, including
xerography, photocopying and recording, or in any information storage
or retrieval system, is forbidden without the written permission of the
publisher, Harlequin Enterprises Limited, 225 Duncan Mill Road,
Don Mills, Ontario, Canada M3B 3K9.

All characters in this book have no existence outside the imagination of
the author and have no relation whatsoever to anyone bearing the same
name or names. They are not even distantly inspired by any individual
known or unknown to the author, and all incidents are pure invention.

This edition published by arrangement with Harlequin Books S.A.

® and TM are trademarks of the publisher. Trademarks indicated with
® are registered in the United States Patent and Trademark Office, the
Canadian Trade Marks Office and in other countries.

Printed in U.S.A.

CHAPTER ONE

SISTER HENRIETTA BRODIE yawned as she climbed the last few treads of the staircase leading to Women's Medical; she had stayed up late the night before, listening, with three other Ward Sisters, to Agnes Bent, who had Men's Medical and was leaving to get married in a few weeks' time and had still to solve the knotty problem of whether to wear a hat or a veil at her wedding. She was a girl of gentle nature, easily swayed by other opinions, and the argument had gone on until after midnight. Henrietta had rather enjoyed it; she liked Agnes, who was pretty enough to wear whatever she fancied and look lovely, but the others had been divided in their opinions, so that the discussion, prolonged with several pots of tea, had gone on for longer than she had bargained for, and when she had at last got to bed, it was to lie awake until the small hours.

Agnes' happy chatter had reminded her that she was going to be twenty-nine in a week's time, and what was worse, she had recently refused Roger Thorpe, the chief pharmacist at St Clement's, for the second time, and she didn't think that he would ask her again. If she had had any relatives to advise her, they would probably have told her that she had been silly to have given up the chance of marrying such a worthy man—her own age, steady and serious and hard-working. And so dull, added Henrietta to herself. Roger hadn't been the first man to ask her to marry him, but he could possibly be the last.

She had sat up in bed at three o'clock in the morning, struck by the sobering thought that twenty-nine was only a year from thirty. Had she been foolish? Roger had all the makings of a good husband, and yet, she had reflected, he had accepted her refusal with a lukewarm regret; he might have been disappointed, but he hadn't been heartbroken. Her tired mind registered that fact while it had wondered in a nebulous fashion if she would ever meet a man who was neither too worthy nor dull, and who, if she were fool enough to refuse him, would follow her ruthlessly until she changed her mind—he would have to be rich, because she was poor, and good-looking, and because she was tall and well built, he would have to be bigger than she was... She had slid back against the pillow, and slept on the idea.

She remembered it all very clearly now as she crossed the landing to her office, her ears registering the various ward sounds; the breakfast things being collected on to the trolleys, the swish of the curtains as the nurses started to draw them round the beds, the metallic clink of bedpans from the far end of the ward and Mrs Pim's shrill old voice calling: 'Nurse, Nurse!' just as she always did after each and every breakfast. But nothing untoward—Henrietta nodded to herself and opened the office door.

The night nurses were waiting for her, and so was her staff nurse, Joan Legg. She wished them good morning in her quiet, pretty voice, and sat down at her desk. The Kardex was open at the first patient's name, ready for her to read, but instead she asked: 'Did you have a good night, Nurse Cutts? That new case—Miss Crow—was the sedation enough or do you want a bigger dose for tonight?'

She looked up and smiled at the student nurse she was talking to, and the smile lighted the whole of her lovely face. Henrietta might be eight or nine years older than her companions, but it was difficult to see that. She was a tall girl, built on generous lines without being plump, with a creamy skin and dark hair curling gently which she pinned up ruthlessly into a bun. Her mouth was kind as well as generously curved and her eyes were dark and thickly lashed. The student nurse, meeting their inquiring gaze and knowing all about the

chief pharmacist, thought it a good thing that Sister
Brodie had refused him. She was too dishy to be
wasted on anyone so ordinary; she ought to marry
someone dramatic—tall and dark and a little
wicked...

'Nurse?' Henrietta's voice was inquiring, and
Cutts abandoned her ideas for her superior's future
happiness and plunged into a businesslike account
of the night's work.

When the night nurses had gone, Henrietta got
up, rearranged her frilled muslin cap before the
tiny mirror, tweaked the bow under her chin to a
more dignified angle and went to look out of the
window. 'Now let's see,' she said, 'there's the barium meal at ten and three X-rays, and Mrs Pim to
persuade to go down to Physio—get them started
on the bed-baths, will you, Legg? I'll be out in a
minute.' She glanced at her watch, 'God won't be
here until half past ten, but we'd better be ready
by ten if we can manage it.'

She was referring to the senior consultant, Sir
Cuthbert Cornish, whose day it was to do a ward
round. He was a peppery man, very tall and thin,
with a booming voice which reduced the younger
nurses to a state of mindless jelly; a bedside manner which charmed his patients and a confirmed
opinion that he was always right. He nearly always
was; Henrietta liked him, and not being afraid of

his loud voice, treated him with a sangfroid which he enjoyed. She went and sat down again after Staff had gone and sorted through the patients' notes and X-rays, refreshing her memory, for God, while permitting her to speak her mind when it concerned the patients or the ward, would brook no slipshod treatment; he expected the right answer when he asked a question.

Presently she got up once more and went into the ward, a little pile of letters and parcels in her hand; it killed two birds with one stone, giving out the post and having a short chat with each patient as she did her round. It took quite a long time, but she never tried to hurry it, some of the women had few visitors and almost no post; they needed to talk even if only for five minutes, the other, luckier ones, with large families to visit them and letters every day, took up only a few minutes of her time, but even so, with thirty patients the round took an hour and sometimes longer, with constant interruptions, small emergencies and the occasional early visit from a doctor. This morning, however, there were few interruptions to take up her time. She went from bed to bed, finding time to keep an eye on the running of the ward as she did so, and by the time she had reached old Mrs Pim in the last bed by the door, the morning's routine was nicely started—even if God came early they would be ready for him. Henrietta dispatched the cases to X-Ray, sent a nurse down with the barium meal, who was a nervous woman and would probably be sick when she got there anyway, sent the first of the student nurses to their coffee break and went back into her office.

Legg knocked on the door a minute later. 'Coffee, Sister?' she asked. 'Everything's going nicely.'

Henrietta nodded. 'Bring a cup for you,' she invited as she picked up a letter addressed to herself from the desk. Sam, the porter, must have brought it up when he came for the stores list; he knew that on round days she had no chance to leave the ward to collect her post from the nurses' home. She turned it over idly; it looked official and as it was typed, she had no idea from whom it might be, only that the postmark was London. She slipped it into her pocket, to be read later on when the round was over.

Sir Cuthbert Cornish arrived early; usually he was late but just now and again he turned up at least twenty minutes too soon, presumably in the hope that no one would be ready for him and he would be able to complain, but Henrietta had been Ward Sister for some years now and was up to his tricks; he was met, as always, by his registrar, his houseman, the social worker and the girl from

Physio, with her a yard or so in front, so that he might be greeted in the correct way, and Staff lurking discreetly in the background, reinforced by a student nurse ready to do any of the odd jobs the great man might think up. Today, however, he was in a genial mood; the round went well with a few setbacks and a kind of interval half way up the ward while he told Henrietta a funny story. The round done at last, they parted on the best of terms at the ward door, and while his little procession made its way to Men's Medical on the other side of the block, Henrietta went back into the ward, where the dinner trolley, concealed in the kitchen, had been rushed into place ready for her to serve the patients' dinners. She doled out steamed fish, diabetic diets and stew for the well ones, while she and Staff conned over the round. She had made notes from time to time, but most of God's instructions she held in her head; after their own dinner she and Legg would go to her office during the visiting hour and go over the notes together so that his orders—and they had been many—might be carried out to the letter.

Henrietta didn't remember her letter until the visitors had gone and the patients were having tea. The ward was almost quiet, with only two nurses keeping an eye on its occupants while the rest of the staff went to their own tea. Legg had gone off duty at half past two and would be back at half past six to relieve her. She looked out of the window at the grey dreary January afternoon, trying to make up her mind if she would go out that evening or go to bed early—bed would be nice, she decided as she drew the Kardex towards her and began the bare bones of the day report so that Legg could fill it in later, but she pushed it aside when Florrie, the ward maid, came in with her tea; a good excuse to take a few minutes off, she told herself, and at the same time remembered her letter.

She opened it without much curiosity and paused to sip her tea before she read it. It was from a firm of solicitors, informing her that her aunt, Miss Henrietta Brodie, had died a week previously and that, by the terms of her will, she, her niece and sole surviving relative, was to inherit the property known as Dam 3 in the village of Gijzelmortel, situated in the province of North Brabant, Holland, together with its contents and such moneys as remained after the payment of certain legacies. The writer begged her to pay him a visit at the earliest opportunity and remained hers faithfully, Jeremy Boggett, of Messrs Boggett, Payne, Boggett and Boggett.

Henrietta read this exciting information through a second time, looked at the back and then the envelope to make sure that she had missed nothing and then laid it down on the desk and drank her tea. Her first reaction was that she was dreaming, to be quickly supplanted by the idea that it was a mistake. She had had an Aunt Henrietta, true enough, a vague relative she had never seen and whom her parents, when they had been alive, never mentioned. She had presumed her dead for years and had never known where she had lived or anything about her. She poured herself another cup of tea and lifted the telephone receiver; private calls were not allowed from the hospital, but this, she considered, justified breaking that rule. She dialled the number engraved on the letter, not quite believing that anyone would answer her—but they did; an efficient feminine voice, enquiring what might be done for her, and when she asked rather uncertainly if she might see Mr Jeremy Boggett the following morning and gave her name, the voice asked her to hold the line, and after a few minutes an elderly man's voice, owned presumably by that gentleman, assured her that he would be glad to see her at her earliest convenience and would ten o'clock suit her?

Henrietta put the receiver down and reread the letter while a number of exciting ideas raced round inside her head. A house of her own—she could go and stay...and money too, perhaps enough to allow her to give up nursing for a while. After all, she could always get another job when the money had run out. The prospect was tempting; she would see what the solicitor had to say and then go and see Miss Brice, the Principal Nursing Officer. Meanwhile there was her work to get on with. She put the letter into her pocket and drew the Kardex towards her.

She wasn't on until one o'clock the next day, time enough to go to the solicitor's office, have a snack in a coffee shop somewhere and be on duty on time, and because it was a fine morning, though cold, and she had time on her hands, she walked for the half hour needed to get her from the hospital to Lincoln's Inn. Messrs Boggett, Payne, Boggett and Boggett had an office on the top floor of a narrow Georgian house: Henrietta climbed the stairs, the letter clutched in her hand as a kind of talisman, still not quite believing it.

It was true, however. Mr Jeremy Boggett, surely the senior partner, she thought irrelevantly, for he was white-haired and whiskered and very, very old, offered a chair and applied himself to the task of reading her aunt's will.

The house was indeed hers. 'A snug little property, Miss Brodie, but small—furnished, of course, and extremely economical in upkeep.' He peered at her over his glasses and smiled. 'I believe, from your aunt's letter sent to me just before her death, that you have no relatives, in which case it will be doubly pleasant for you to have a home of your own, although you are quite free to do what you wish with the property. Sell it, perhaps?'

Henrietta shook her head. 'Oh, no—that's the last thing I would wish to do. I haven't had much time to think about it, but I like the idea of going there for a little while—to live, you know.'

He glanced down at the papers in his hand. 'That is quite possible of course. I do not know how you are placed financially, Miss Brodie, but as far as we can calculate at the moment, your aunt left only a small sum of money—about six hundred pounds—which will be advanced to you should you require it.'

It sounded a great deal, even in these days; if she were careful she would be able to live there, if she liked it, for quite a long time; there would be no rent and if she were desperate at the end of that time she could always get herself a job and let the house besides. 'Are there any extras to pay?' she wanted to know. 'Rates and things like that,' she added vaguely.

Mr Boggett consulted his papers once more. 'Certainly, but the village is rural and the rates are low, I imagine that an outlay of fifty pounds or so annually would cover them.'

Henrietta was doing rapid sums in her head. She

had a little money saved, she was young and strong and could get a job whenever she needed one. She drew a breath and smiled at the old man. 'You know, I think I'll arrange to go over and stay there for a while—if I like it very much perhaps I could stay—you see, there's nothing to keep me here.'

He nodded in agreement. 'I believe your decision would have made your aunt very happy.' He took off his glasses and polished them. 'It is a long time since I last saw Miss Brodie, she went to live in Holland many years ago now, but she always wrote charming letters.' He coughed. 'I shall be happy to help you in any way, Miss Brodie. The estate is a small one and once we have arranged things with the Dutch authorities and so forth, it should be a simple matter to clear the matter up within a few weeks. Perhaps you will let me know when you wish to go and I will do my best to have everything in order by then. The money is in Holland, naturally. I take it that you would wish it to be left where it is, in the bank.'

'Oh, please. I'll be able to get it out?'

'Yes, I will arrange for you to have a letter to present to the manager. You are unacquainted with the Dutch language?'

'I daresay there'll be someone there who speaks English? I expect I'll pick up enough Dutch to get by once I'm there.' She paused. 'I suppose my aunt didn't leave me a letter, or—or anything?'

'I'm afraid not. She had seen you only once or twice, I believe, when you were a baby, but she seems to have retained an affection for you. Blood,' observed Mr Boggett, 'is thicker than water.'

Perhaps her aunt had been glad to have someone to whom she could leave her home; it struck Henrietta with some force that she herself had no one.

Too excited to drink more than a cup of coffee, she took an extravagant taxi back to St Clement's and went at once to see Miss Brice. It was unusual for anyone to demand an interview at such short notice; the Admin. Sisters, sitting at their desks in the outer office, tried to fob her off with an appointment for the next day, but Henrietta, uplifted by the knowledge that she was now a woman of property, however small, and had means of her own, even smaller, refused to be put off. She walked into Miss Brice's office, feeling a little top-heavy with excitement and looking twice as pretty as she normally did because of it.

Miss Brice blinked at her Ward Sister's blinding good looks, wishing to herself that she could look the same, and inquired as to the reason for Henrietta's urgency. She listened while it was explained to her and only when it was finished did she say: 'You appear to have made up your mind rather quickly, Sister. You are quite sure about it? You have a splendid job here with a good chance of promotion later on, and forgive me for saying so, but you tell me that you have no relatives, and in such circumstances surely it would be better for you to remain in secure employment?'

'I've been in secure employment since I started nursing, ten years ago,' Henrietta reminded her. 'Ten years,' she repeated with faint bitterness, 'and I've not so much as gone on a day trip to Boulogne. I do not wish to be secure, Miss Brice.'

Miss Brice looked startled. 'Well—I really don't know what to say, Sister Brodie. I certainly can't prevent you from doing something you wish to do. You say that you have two weeks' holiday left from this year? Supposing you take those and let me know your decision during that period? You will, of course, have to forfeit your salary if you leave on those terms, and I hope that you will allow a reasonable time to elapse before taking your holiday.'

Henrietta was on her feet. 'Would a month be long enough?' she asked. 'If I could have my holiday in one month's time and then let you know about leaving—I shall know more about it by then.'

Miss Brice could lose gracefully when she had

to. 'That will suit me very well, Sister. If you do decide to give up your post you do realize that I shall fill it immediately? If you should, at some future date, apply for a post here, I shall always be pleased to consider you for it, though I must warn you that it might not be exactly what you wished for.' She bowed her elegantly capped head in dismissal, and Henrietta, with a suitable murmur, almost danced from the room.

She went on duty looking much as usual. Certainly her manner was as calm and assured as it always was, only her fine eyes sparkled whenever she allowed herself to think of her changed future, but in the Sisters' sitting room at tea time, she told her news to those of her friends who were sharing tea and buttered toast round the electric fire, and it was received with gratifying surprise and a good deal of speculation as well as instant requests to be invited to stay, and unlike Miss Brice, they agreed wholeheartedly that in her shoes they would have done exactly the same thing. 'And probably,' said a voice, 'Miss Brice would have done the same if she'd been twenty years younger,' a remark which gave rise to a short pause while everyone there thought how awful it must be to be as old as Miss Brice; fifty if she was a day.

'How are you going, and when?' asked someone else.

'Well, I haven't a clue at the moment how to go,' said Henrietta thoughtfully, 'though I shall take Charlie.' A very old Mini bought from one of the housemen three years previously, it had been second-hand then, and the man at the garage assured her each time she went for petrol that it was a miracle that Charlie went at all. 'At least he'll get me there,' she added.

Whereupon they fell to discussing just what she would need to take with her and became so absorbed in this engrossing subject that they forgot the time and went back to the wards a little late.

The month went quickly; there was a lot to see to—passport, visits to Mr Boggett, Charlie to be overhauled, her few friends to be bidden a temporary farewell—and the ward was extra busy too, so that she was tired enough to sleep soundly each night and not lie awake wondering if she had been rash, exchanging a steady, safe life for an unknown one. True, she had read up a great deal about Holland, she knew exactly where the village of Gijzelmortel lay, even though she hadn't an idea how to pronounce it, and she had bought a phrase book which she hoped would get her over the first few weeks. She had drawn some of her savings from the bank too, for it seemed logical that if she were going to change her life, she should change her wardrobe too. She bought a tweed suit in a pleasing shade of brown which went very well with her last year's coat and she bought, amongst other things, a pair of sensible lined boots. They struck her as unfashionable, but if it were cold—and there was, after all, a good deal of winter left—she might be glad of them; the guide book had said that it could be cold in Holland and that skating was a national pastime, which led her to believe that there might be degrees of coldness, for it wasn't a national pastime in England.

The guide book also advised the taking of cosmetics just in case one couldn't buy that particular brand, so she stocked up lavishly and had her collection topped by a large bottle of Dioressence given to her by her friends. And being a practical girl she packed candles and matches and a powerful torch and enough food to keep her going for a day or so. Presumably there would be a village shop, and she would have Charlie, if he was still on his wheels, to take her to the neighbouring towns. She wondered uneasily about garages, but surely every village had one these days—anyway, she mustn't start crossing her bridges until she came to them. She had never understood Charlie's insides; the man at the garage had kept them working, and now it was too late for her to learn anything about them, but that was something she wasn't going to worry about either—she wasn't going to worry about anything, she was going to enjoy herself.

She began her journey on a cold, bleak morning whose sky promised snow before the day was out. She had booked on the Dover ferry and planned to arrive on the other side of the Channel in the early afternoon so that she would have several hours of daylight in which to travel. The ferry was almost empty and the sea was rough. Henrietta sat uneasily, hoping that she wouldn't be sick, her eyes averted from the weather outside, and presently she slept for a little while and when she woke and staggered down below to tidy herself it was to hear that because of the rough weather they would be docking at least an hour late. She got herself a cup of tea and settled down to read, only to cast her book down and con her map once more, making sure that she knew the route she had to take. It looked an alarmingly long way, although she knew that once she landed at Zeebrugge it was barely forty miles to Breskens where she would have to take the ferry across the river Schold, and once at Vlissingen, it was only a little more than seventy miles. It would be well after two when they landed, she calculated, and it was dark by five o'clock, so provided she could get to Vlissingen by then it should be easy enough. It was towards her journey's end that she would have to be careful not to miss the side road which would take her to Gijsz-elmortel. There was a landmark on the map, a castle, but in the dark she doubted if that would be of much use to her. She folded the map, determined not to get worried, aware that she would be glad when she was safely there.

It was sleeting when they docked, and bitter cold. Henrietta, one of the first away, drove carefully along the coast road which would lead her to the border town of Sluis and Holland. There was almost no traffic, something she was grateful for; the dark sky was closing in rapidly now and she could see that the hours of daylight she had reckoned on were to be considerably shortened. She ignored her desire to get as much out of Charlie as possible; the roads were treacherous and there were signposts to look out for as well as remembering to drive on the other side of the road.

She pressed on steadily, through the Customs post at Sluis and on to Breskens where the ferry was waiting. She breathed a sigh of relief as she got out of her little car and climbed the narrow iron stairs to the deck above. There was a brightly lit saloon there and a coffee bar at one end of it, doing a roaring trade. Henrietta pointed at what she wanted, handed over a note, received a handful of change and found herself a table where she drank her coffee, ate her cheese roll and examined the money. It seemed small, although when she looked at it carefully she could see that it was similar to the money at home, only the tiny silver coins were different. She stowed them away now that she had had something to eat. Her cheerful mood lasted as she drove off the ferry and took the N97, which would take her to Breda without any complications. She encouraged Charlie to a steady forty-five and kept doggedly on. Sleet was still falling, but the motorway was wide and well surfaced and she was a good driver, so in due time she found herself on the roundabout outside that city and heaved another sigh of relief. Not very far now and she would be there.

The motorway skirted Tilburg too. Henrietta left it soon after, and in another seven or eight miles saw what she was looking for—the signpost to Gijzelmortel. She turned into the exit point, swung the little car under a flyover and joined a narrow road on the other side, where presently another signpost directed her into a still narrower lane. After that there was no sign, no houses, no lights even, only her headlamps cutting into the sleety darkness. She should be there, she told herself, and discovered that she was, for there was the village sign on the side of the road and a few yards further she saw the first house. The road curved away to the left and she followed it, to discover that the village—and Mr Boggett had been quite right, it was very small—was a mere circle of houses round a cobbled square with a bandstand in its centre. There were one or two narrow lanes leading away from it, but he had told her that the house was in the centre of the village. She slowed the car to a crawl round the square, cheered by the sight of the lighted windows around her, and presently reached a massive gateway, with lanterns on its brick posts, and just a few yards further on a row of tiny houses. There was a wall plaque on the first one with Dam written on it. The third house along was number three. She was there!

CHAPTER TWO

HENRIETTA took the house key from her handbag and got out of the car, savouring the moment despite the sneering wind and sleet, so sluggish now that it was almost snow. Oblivious of these discomforts, she stood back to survey her property—a very little house in the middle of a row of six similar dwellings, all exactly alike, built of bricks with one large window beside a solid front door and another window above, crowded into its steeply gabled roof. She stood a little further back and by peering beyond the lights above the gateway was able to see another row, exactly similar beyond the further gate post. Possibly a park, she speculated, for the wrought iron gates were open. The sight of them triggered off a highly improbable daydream, in which she saw herself on a hot summer's day, roaming its greenness, possibly with a dog… A nasty little flurry of snowy wind took her breath and brought the daydream to an abrupt end and she crossed the narrow flagged pavement and turned the key in the lock.

The hall was a tiny square from which the stairs ascended steeply, and there was a door on the right.

Henrietta shone her torch and found the light switch and pressed it, but nothing happened—she had half expected that, although she had hoped that she wouldn't need the candles which she had thoughtfully brought with her. She went back to Charlie and carried in her overnight bag and her case; to get to the candles was the first necessity.

The house seemed all at once warmer by reason of the small flame; she opened the door and with the candle held high, went inside. The dining-room, she judged, nicely furnished with an old-fashioned round table and pretty Victorian chairs; there was a small sideboard too and pictures on the walls, but she left these for the moment and went into the room beyond—without doubt the sitting room, as small as the dining-room and even in the chilly dimness, cosy, its armchairs with shabby covers drawn up on either side of an old-fashioned iron stove, a couple of small lamp tables, another chair or two and one wall almost entirely taken up by an upright piano. There was a window and door on the third wall; presumably the back garden was beyond, but she turned away from the bleak darkness outside and opened the door to the kitchen. Small, too, as was to be expected but as far as she could see by the light of the wavering candle flame, adequately equipped; a sink with a geyser above it, a small table with two gas rings and shelves of saucepans and cooking utensils. She put down her candle carefully and tried the geyser hopefully, but there was no gas, neither was there any water when she turned on the tap.

She went back to the hall, looking for the meters, retracing her steps slowly without success. She was kneeling in the kitchen again, peering hopefully under the sink, when she heard someone enter the house. She got to her feet slowly, her heart beating an uneasy tattoo, eyeing the man who was standing at the kitchen door, looking at her. She was a big girl, but he more than matched her for size—a head taller for a start and with broad shoulders, massive in a sheepskin jacket, and as far as she could see in the dim light, exceedingly handsome. She waited uncertainly; she had been a fool to have left the front door on the latch, but probably he was just a casual passer-by. She said coolly: 'I have no idea who you are, but this is my house and I must ask you to leave it.'

He came right into the kitchen. 'A very hoity-toity speech,' he remarked in an English as perfect as her own, 'quite wasted on me and useless to anyone else around here—they wouldn't have understood a word of it.'

'Who are you?' She stood her ground although the instinct to move back was strong, but she was annoyed at being called hoity-toity, so that she lifted her pretty, determined chin and looked down her fine nose at him.

'Your landlord.' He laughed without amusement and she said at once:

'You're mistaken, this house is mine. My aunt, Miss Brodie, left it to me.'

He sighed loudly. 'I have neither the time nor the patience to mull over the intricacies of lease-hold property. Take my word for it that I own the lease of this house, Miss Henrietta Brodie.'

She gave him a startled glance. How had he known her name was Henrietta? she longed to ask, but instead, 'You still haven't told me who you are,' she reminded him coldly.

For some reason this amused him. 'Van Hessel—Marnix van Hessel.'

'And how did you know that I was here?'

'My dear good young woman, this is a very small village. Willemse the greengrocer was putting his van away when he saw you arrive—he came to tell my housekeeper, who told me. In a community of this size we all tend to mind each other's business.'

She was annoyed again. 'Or indulge your curiosity.'

His eyes—grey, she thought, but wasn't sure—narrowed. 'You have a nasty sharp tongue,' he observed. 'I am not in the least curious about you—

why should I be? But since it was I who ordered
the electricity and gas and water to be turned off,
it seemed that the least I could do was to come
and turn them on again.'

He stood quite still, staring at her, and after a
moment or two she said awkwardly: 'Well, thank
you…I should be glad…it is a little chilly…'

He gave a short laugh. 'It's damned cold.' He
walked past her into the scullery and she was
aware once more of his great size as he bent to go
through the door. She stood still, holding the candle aloft while he opened a cupboard high up on
the wall. 'Try the lights,' he advised her.

The little kitchen sprang into instant view and
she looked around her with relief and a good deal
of interest, but she was given no time in which to
indulge her curiosity. 'Turn on the gas,' he com-
manded. That worked too, and so, presently, did
the water. Tea, thought Henrietta, a hot water bottle and bed, while aloud she said civilly: 'Thank
you very much, I can…' She was interrupted.

'I'll get the stove going, there should be coal
and wood outside.'

She tried again. 'Please don't bother, I shall…'
and was silenced by his: 'Of course it's a bother,
but I wouldn't leave a dog to shiver to death on a
night like this.'

She bristled, her dark eyes sparkling with tem-

per. She said in a voice made high by her strong
feelings: 'I'm obliged to you for your help, Mr van
Hessel, but I can manage very well—don't let me
keep you.'

He flung open the back door, his torch cutting a
swathe through the blackness outside, the icy wind
rushing in to set her shivering again. 'Don't be a
fool,' he said pleasantly as he went out. 'Go upstairs and unpack.'

Over the years of being without a family she had
achieved a fine independence, so it was all the
more surprising to her to find herself climbing a
miniature staircase with her overnight bag. There
were two bedrooms, she discovered, with a large
landing between them. They faced front and back
and she chose the back room, pleased with the sim-
plicity of its furnishings; a narrow bed, a chest of
drawers with a mirror above it, a basket chair, well
cushioned, and bright rugs on the polished floor.
The curtains, she noted as she pulled them to, were
shabby now, but the fabric had once been good.
The other room was almost identical; she pulled
the curtains here too and lingered to explore the
landing. There was a cupboard built into one of its
walls, full, she discovered to her delight, to its brim
with bed linen, blankets and everything she could
need for the house, there were even two old-
fashioned eiderdowns, a little faded but whole.

Henrietta sighed with deep satisfaction and went back downstairs.

Mr van Hessel might be an ill-tempered man, but he was handy at lighting a stove. It was crackling well and already its heat was taking the sharp chill off the room. There was a scuttle of coals too and as she entered he came in with an armful of small logs which he stacked tidily in a corner. When he had done this, he stood up, studying her in a cool way which annoyed her very much. 'You look as though you could do with a good hot supper,' he observed.

'I stopped on my way here.' She had spoken too quickly and he had seen that. He moved to the door. 'And that's a lie if ever I heard one,' he told her, 'but as it's obviously intended to warn me off inviting you to a meal, I'll take the hint. Good night.'

He had gone, and the room looked bare without him. She went into the kitchen, found the kettle and put it on to boil for a cup of tea while she considered her visitor—a large, domineering man, used to giving orders and getting his own way, and if he owned the lease of the house, why hadn't Mr Boggett told her about him? She knew very little about ground rents and such things. She wondered now, a little uneasily, if she would be able to afford to pay it. Presumably she would have to ask Mr van Hessel how much it was. It seemed likely that she would see him again; he must live close by, for he had come—and gone—on foot. Perhaps he lived on the other side of the square where the houses, as she had passed them in the dark, had appeared larger, though it was hard to imagine him in a small village house.

She made the tea and rooted through her stores for a tin of baked beans and a packet of soup; a proper hot supper would have been nice, she thought wistfully, but he had offered it in much the same way as he might have offered a bone to a hungry dog. She ate her beans, drained the teapot and went upstairs to make her bed. It wasn't late, but she was longing for sleep; she went downstairs again, made up the stove, had a shower in the tiny cubicle squeezed into the scullery, and went to her bed with both eiderdowns on top of her and a hot water bottle as well.

It wasn't quite light when she woke, although her watch told her that it was eight o'clock. She got up and drew back the curtains to see what lay behind the house; a garden, small and brick-walled to a height of six feet, a mere plot of neglected grass with a tangle of rose bushes in one corner. The scullery roof was just below her window and beyond that there was a brick lean-to shed, where presumably her visitor of the night before had found the coal. But beyond that she could see very little; identical sized gardens on either side of her, incredibly neat, and a dense row of conifers, screening whatever lay beyond the back walls of the row of little houses. She would find out, she promised herself, dressing rapidly in sweater and slacks before going down to rake out the stove and make it up again and to the kitchen to get her breakfast. Tea and porridge and tinned milk; presently she would find the village shop. She washed up, made her bed, found her phrase book and, warmly wrapped against the weather, opened her front door. Charlie was still parked outside; she would have to find a garage for him very soon. She ran a woollen-mitted hand over his icy roof and jumped when Mr van Hessel said from behind her, 'Yours, I presume.' And when she wheeled round to face him: 'I take it you believe in travelling on a prayer—your faith must be very strong if you pin it to this—er—car.'

'Charlie is a splendid little car,' she told him with dignity. 'He may not look quite—well...' she paused, unable to think of the right word. 'He suits me,' she finished with a snap.

Mr van Hessel was studying her once more, his magnificent head, with its dark silvered hair, on one side. 'Charlie,' he remarked reflectively. 'You are a most extraordinary young woman.' He allowed his gaze to ramble from her face down to her sensible boots and back again to meet her indignant eyes. 'You're still young—not yet thirty, I should imagine?' He ignored her angry choke. 'And even in your so suitable winter clothes you are quite unmistakably a woman.'

Her voice would have frozen anyone else. 'I wish you would stop referring to me as a young woman!'

'Ah, is young lady more to your liking?'

'My name is Brodie,' she pointed out.

'Miss Henrietta Brodie—I had not forgotten. Have you a garage for this car?'

'No, I'm just going to see about it.'

His eyes widened with laughter. 'There is no garage in the village and those who have cars use outbuildings and sheds. I cannot think of anyone who could accommodate you. Perhaps you would allow me to house Charlie for the time being at least.'

He was a most extraordinary man, she thought crossly, being rude to her with every other breath and then being helpful—but she had to have a garage. 'Thank you,' she said stiffly, 'I'd be very obliged, just until I can find somewhere permanent.' She gave him a questioning look. 'You have got room?'

He inclined his head. 'Indeed yes. I have also

asked your neighbour to chop wood for you—I daresay he will come this afternoon. He speaks no English, but I expect you will be able to manage.'

'Thank you—how much should I pay him?'

Her companion looked astounded. 'Nothing. He's a neighbour, he would feel insulted. Have you done your shopping?'

'I'm on my way—there must be a shop…'

'A general store, I believe you would call it in English. We will go together, unless of course you have sufficient knowledge of our language to make your purchases?'

She was being overwhelmed with kindness, and yet behind his bland face she thought there was laughter lurking. 'I can't speak a word,' she told him.

They crossed the cobbles, skirted the bandstand and turned a corner into an exceedingly narrow street, crammed with little houses and paved with cobblestones, too. The shop was half way down its length and there were quite a number of women inside, having, from the sound of their voices, a pleasant gossip. They fell silent as Mr van Hessel opened the door and ushered her in, and she had the strange idea that in a bygone age they would have dropped him a curtsey; as it was they chorused with respectful voices and waited to hear what he had to say. Of course Henrietta couldn't understand a word, but he smiled at them as he spoke, and they smiled back, but still with respect, and after a minute of talking he turned to ask: 'How much milk do you want?'

'Oh, a pint each day.'

'You forget, my good...I beg your pardon— Miss Brodie, that we do not have your pints here, only litres. I suggest a litre every other day.'

She nodded. At least he had remembered not to call her his good girl!

'Bread?'

'Well, I thought I'd make my own, but just until I'm settled, yes, please. Can I buy it here?'

'No. The baker comes three times a week, his van is parked in the square and you fetch it for yourself.' He stopped to speak to the woman behind the counter. 'He doesn't come today, but Mevrouw Ros will let you have half a loaf. What else?'

'Bacon...'

'No, most people don't eat your sort of bacon. What else?'

'Eggs, cheese, butter...'

'Butter? That is expensive in Holland, not many people eat it.'

'Oh, well, margarine, I suppose. Where do I buy meat?'

He said something or other to the woman. 'The

butcher comes twice a week, he will be here in half an hour or so—in the square. I will tell Mevrouw Ros that somebody must help you with the money and so on.'

'Don't you mean ask?' she wanted to know. 'You sound like a feudal lord.'

His lips twitched. 'Unpardonable of me,' he murmured. 'Vegetables? Willemse takes his van round every day except Sunday, he comes to the door and you can buy what you want from him. I should point out that we have not moved with the times here, we cling to our old habits. In the big towns and modern villages, the shopping is done much as it is in England—although I imagine that you have not had much experience of that—St Clement's has a large nurses' home, and very likely you lived in.'

She gaped at him. 'However did you know?' she began, to be halted by his impatient: 'Oh, later, later, I have no time now. Do you wish to pay for these things now or will you have an account?'

'I'll pay now, please.'

She opened her purse and handed him the money he asked for and he paid it while she smiled round at the interested faces watching her. 'I didn't realize that it would be so foreign,' she declared as they left the shop.

He had her basket, and from the surprised

glances from the women they passed in the street, he wasn't often seen with a shopping basket. They crossed the square together and at her door she took it from him. 'I should like to see you about the ground rent,' she began. 'Mr Boggett didn't tell me about it. Do I pay you, and how much is it?'

'I haven't the least idea,' he told her blandly. 'We'll look into it some other time.'

'Very well, but I should like to know, so that I can...' She stopped; she wasn't going to tell him that she had to be careful with her money. 'Where do you live?' she asked. 'Perhaps I could come and see you about it.'

He took the basket from her once more and set it down on her doorstep, and without speaking took her arm and walked her to the big gates.

'Here,' he said, and stopped midway between the great pillars. Henrietta hadn't gone that way until now, they had walked to the shop along the other side of the square. She stared before her at the short drive, leading straight as a ruler from the gates, and at its end a square-walled castle, surrounded by a moat. There was a bridge spanning it so that cars could reach its great wooden door exactly facing the open gates, and a sweep of gravel just sufficiently large to allow of them to turn. The castle's whitewashed walls rose straight and solid from the steel-grey water and were capped by a tiled roof like a clown's hat, and there were a great many small windows. On either side of it, half way round the moat and almost out of sight, she could see two smaller bridges, connecting the castle with the drive which encircled the outer edge of the moat. She could think of nothing to say; this then was the castle the guide book had mentioned and which she had mistakenly assumed was a ruin—but this was no ruin, it bore all the signs of care and money lavished upon it, and when she looked around her she saw the coat of arms engraved on each pillar. No wonder the women in the shop had been so polite to Mr van Hessel!

'Are you the lord of the manor?' she wanted to know.

'Well, we don't call it that.' He was amused again.

'But you do own these houses?' She pointed to the neat row of houses on either side of the gates. 'Almshouses, are they?'

'My dear good…Miss Brodie, they are not almshouses—the leasehold is mine, certainly, but the houses are given as gifts, usually for the recipient's lifetime. In your case your aunt's house was given to her together with the right to leave it to any member of her family, should she wish to do so.'

Henrietta stared up at him, wishing she could

read his face; there was a great deal she wanted to know. She had opened her mouth to ask the first question when he said: 'Forgive me, I have an urgent appointment,' and was gone, stalking up the drive to his own front door—from his back she thought it probable that he had forgotten all about her.

She spent the day cleaning her little house, tidying cupboards and polishing furniture. Some of it, she discovered upon closer inspection, was very old and probably valuable. There was a rosewood davenport in the sitting-room, and the dining table was a magnificent example of marquetry, and when she took the loose covers off the easy chairs it was to find that they were upholstered in a rich red velvet, as good as new. She left the covers off and brushed the velvet with care; the little room looked quite beautiful now—she would need flowers, though; she would go to Tilburg in the morning, see the bank manager and give him Mr Boggett's letter and then do a little shopping. She wound the Friesian clock hanging on the dining-room wall and the small carriage clock on the sitting-room mantelpiece and, well satisfied with her work, went to make herself some belated coffee.

She had just finished it when there was a knock on the door; the neighbour, come to chop the wood; there was no doubt of that, for he swung a nasty-looking axe from a hamlike hand. They smiled and nodded in speechless friendliness as she ushered him out to the shed and went back to answer the door once more. One of the women who had been in the shop this time, smiling and pointing across the square where a van had parked. Henrietta remembered the butcher, put on her coat and walked with her guide across the cobbles and bought her meat. It was amazing how one could manage without speaking a word, she reflected, receiving change from the butcher, exchanging smiles and nods from the other customers as she went back across the square to find the greengrocer at the door. And this was even easier; all she had to do was walk round the van pointing to what she wanted and when she had made her choice he kicked off his *klompen* and carried her purchases through into the kitchen for her. Everyone was kind, and it surprised her a little, and Mr van Hessel had been the kindest of them all—which reminded her about Charlie. Perhaps she should give him a clean before he went into the garage Mr van Hessel had offered—and where would that be? she wondered looking about her. Probably through the big gates, but then where? And was she expected to go and find out? She was standing looking up at the grey sky, threatening sleet again, when a small elderly man with a wizened face came rapidly through the gates and stopped beside her. 'Car, miss,' he said, and grinned nicely so that she could have hugged him with relief. 'Oh, good—and you speak English, too.'

He smiled again and nodded. 'I take car, miss.' He put out a hand and she cried: 'Oh, yes, of course you want the key,' and when she had fetched it: 'Where are you taking it?'

But this was beyond him; he shook his head, still smiling, and then asked: 'Tomorrow?'

She nodded urgently. 'Here? Ten o'clock? Or shall I fetch it?'

He hadn't understood, not that part anyway, for he held up two hands to show that he knew what ten meant, saluted her and got into Charlie, who rather surprisingly purred into life and was driven away through the gates and out of sight. Henrietta went back indoors; the arrangements would do for the moment, but once she had got her bearings she would find a shed or something—supposing she wanted Charlie in a hurry, how was she to get him? It was a pity, but she could see that there were a great many questions she would have to ask Mr van Hessel when she saw him again.

She made tea for the neighbour and had a cup herself, deciding to skip lunch, for there was still the linen cupboard to go through. She would get a stew going and eat it later round the stove. The

man went presently and she went to see what he
had done; the logs had been split and piled tidily,
and besides that he had chopped a pile of kindling.
She took some logs back with her, made up the
stove and settled down to her task. It proved a
more lengthy one than she had imagined; Aunt
Harriet had had a remarkably well stocked linen
cupboard, and everything was of the best quality.
Henrietta, happily counting and checking, came to
the conclusion that she would have no need to buy
a single article for years to come.

She finished at last and went downstairs, well
content, to sit in the lamplit room with a tray of
tea and a book while the stew bubbled appetiz-
ingly. After supper she would make a few lists and
try to get her finances planned, but after supper she
found herself thinking of bed; she tidied away the
remains of her meal, had a shower and made herself a cup of cocoa to drink by the stove. She had
enjoyed her day, she thought sleepily, and tomorrow would be fun, too—besides, once she had been
to the bank she would know exactly how much
money she had.

She took her mug out to the sink and went
yawning through the little house, to pause and
straighten a picture on the dining-room wall. It had
caught on something behind it and when she un-
hooked it she saw the small knob on the wall. She

pulled it idly and a little cupboard door, papered over, opened. It was a little high for her, tall though she was, so she got a chair and climbed on it to peer inside. There were several rolls of green baize and a velvet-covered box. She carried them to the light and opened them—there was table silver, simple and old and she supposed valuable. There was a small silver coffee pot too with a cream jug and a sugar bowl, just as simple in design and very beautiful. Henrietta set them down beside the other silver and opened the box. There was a garnet necklace inside; a gold chain, very thick and solid, the garnets fashioned into a cascade of flowers; it shone and glowed in her hands and she wondered who had worn it. She would have to tell someone, she decided as she wrapped everything up again; it might make a difference to the estate, for they were valuable. And who was she to tell? Mr Boggett, perhaps, or the bank manager in Tilburg? She went slowly up to bed, wondering why Aunt Henrietta had hidden them away, and who had given her such a lovely necklace.

She was up early the next morning and although it was still only half light saw with a sinking heart that it had been snowing, and still was. The road to Tilburg was a good one; it was the few kilometres from the village to that road which worried her. True, there were no hills or S-bends and it had

been dark when she had driven along it, but it was
very narrow and the surface was bad. She ate her
breakfast, tidied up the house, peeled potatoes to
go with the rest of the stew and checked her small
stock of tins for a pudding to go after it, then went
upstairs to put on her outdoor clothes; the tweed
coat, while not quite the height of fashion, was
warm and so were the boots, she added a fur bonnet too—an extravagance she had permitted herself
and was now thankful for; it framed her pretty face
attractively and its dark fur was undoubtedly becoming.

It was almost ten o'clock as she opened her front
door, but there was no sign of Charlie; indeed,
there was no sign of anything or anyone, everyone
who could was undoubtedly snug indoors on such
a day. The Catholic church played its carillon for
ten o'clock and the Protestant church, not to be
outdone, chimed the hour with its deliberate, deep
bell, and Henrietta peered round the door once
more. A car was turning out of the castle gates,
not her Mini, but a gleaming, silver-grey Rolls-
Royce, moving silently and disdainfully through
the snow. It drew up before her door and Mr van
Hessel got out.

'You can't take your car out on a day like this,'
he greeted her, without as much as a 'good day'

for politeness' sake. 'I have to go into Tilburg, you may come with me.'

He was standing in the snow, nattily dressed in what she recognized as town clothes of the finest quality, sober grey and exquisitely tailored.

'How do I get back?' she asked; if he wasn't civil enough to wish her good morning she saw no reason to be polite herself.

'Will four o'clock suit you?' he asked carelessly. 'I'll show you where I'll pick you up. Come along, I'm a little late already.'

She locked the door behind her and got in wordlessly; anyone would think, listening to him, that she was to blame for his lateness. She fastened her seat belt and pretended to herself that driving in a Rolls was something she did so often that it no longer gave her a thrill.

The big car made light of the slippery road and she was secretly thankful that she hadn't had to drive Charlie. It wasn't until they had joined the motorway to Tilburg that she spoke. 'How did you know that I was going out at ten o'clock—and to Tilburg?'

'Jan told me. He fetched your car yesterday and I supposed it would be Tilburg—it's the nearest town and I daresay you have business there.'

'With the bank—my aunt's bank—I daresay you

know that too,' she said with a touch of temper. 'You knew my aunt?'

'Yes, very well.'

'Then when you have the time to spare, I have a number of questions I should like to ask you about her.'

'I seldom have time to spare, so you had better start now.'

'Did you know that there's a cupboard in the dining-room of my little house, with silver in it and a necklace?'

'Yes, I knew.'

'Well—is it a secret? Why didn't Mr Boggett tell me about it? Or you, for that matter.'

'I imagine Mr Boggett didn't know, and as for myself, I felt sure that you would find them sooner or later. They're yours now, of course.'

'But are they? Who gave them to Aunt Henrietta in the first place—and I want to know why she lived in Gijzelmortel for so many years and why my parents always allowed me to believe that she was dead—did she do something awful?'

His voice sounded patient enough, although she didn't think he was. 'My uncle gave them to her— no, my dear good girl, do not interrupt. He gave her the house too, to live in for the rest of her life and to leave to anyone she wished. You see, they loved each other; he met her when they were both quite young and was already married, and not happily. They didn't have an affair in the usual sense of that word; it wasn't until she was forty or so that he finally persuaded her to go and live near him. My aunt had become almost impossible to live with by then, leading her own life, not caring for anyone but herself; he desperately needed someone to love, so Henrietta gave in at last and made her home in Gijzelmortel. He furnished the house for her and bought her trifles, and although they loved each other very deeply they were never more than friends—the village loved her; so did anyone who met her. If my aunt had died, they would undoubtedly have married, but my uncle died first and my aunt went to Switzerland to live, but your aunt stayed in her little house because my uncle would have wished it. When my aunt died I came to the castle to live.' He slowed the big car as they neared Tilburg. 'Will you be all right at the bank?'

'Yes, thank you. Do you want me to be there at four o'clock?'

'Outside the bank? Yes. If I am late I will let them know, they can send someone out to tell you.'

Henrietta said 'thank you' meekly, bursting with questions about Aunt Henrietta and not daring to ask them. He had told her the story—just the facts with no trimmings—and supposed that she would be content with that; besides, he wanted to get to his work. She wondered what he did for a living, or perhaps he didn't do anything, just lived in his splendid castle and dabbled on the Stock Exchange.

He slowed the Rolls to a halt and got out to open her door, something she hadn't expected of him. 'Four o'clock,' he reminded her austerely, and had got back in and driven away before she could even thank him.

The visit to the bank was a leisurely business. Henrietta was given coffee while her affairs were explained to her and she left feeling on top of the world, for there was a little more money in her legacy than old Mr Boggett had thought; she would be able to stay in Holland for some time provided she was careful. And she wanted to stay; it was wonderful to have a little house and be independent. When the weather improved she would explore the country around the village, keeping Charlie for a weekly trip to Tilburg or Breda, and she would learn the language and take up piano playing once more; there were endless reasons why she should want to stay, but the main reason she didn't admit to herself, although she was well aware of it lurking at the back of her mind; she wanted to get to know Mr van Hessel—not that she liked him, domineering and bad-tempered as he was, but he was interesting…

Her thoughts nicely occupied, she made her way to the shops, where she resisted the temptation to spend her money on some Italian shoes which caught her fancy, as well as some exquisite gloves and a quantity of delicate undies, which, while wildly expensive, were wholly to her taste. Instead she shopped for wool to knit more gloves, canvas and embroidery silks to occupy her of an evening, a tin of yeast in case the village shop didn't stock it, and an English newspaper. She spent a long time looking in the florists' windows too, but the delicate narcissi and the vivid tulips and hyacinths were too much for her pocket, so she consoled herself with the purchase of several packets of seeds, so that when summer came she would at least have something colourful growing in the garden. All this done, she found a small neat café in a side street and lunched, at the waiter's suggestion, off *erwtensoep*, which she discovered was a tasty meal in itself, being a thick pea soup with pork and sausage in it. She eked this out with a roll and butter and a cup of coffee, and well fortified against the snowy cold, went back to her window-shopping, and when she was tempted to have tea at one of the fashionable tea-shops she passed, reminded herself that she would have to wait for a week or

two before she splashed out too lavishly; she still
didn't know the price of everything and how much
it would cost to live. She contented herself with
another look at the shops and then, in the gathering
gloom of the bleak day, went to meet Mr van Hessel.

He was punctual; the carillons had barely finished their tinkling reminder of the hour when the
Rolls pulled up at the pavement's edge and he
opened the door for her to get in. It was deliciously
warm inside and Henrietta sank back into the fra-
grant leather with a little sigh. The journey back
to Gijzelmortel wouldn't take long, but there
would be time enough for her companion to answer a few more questions. But in this she was to
be disappointed; Mr van Hessel didn't want to talk,
that was plain from the start; to her cheerful remarks about the shops she had seen he gave nothing more than a grunt, and after a minute or two,
when she tried again about the weather, he didn't
even bother to grunt. A rude man, she told herself,
and peeped at him. A tired man, too; she didn't
know how old he was—forty, perhaps—but his
handsome face showed every line and his dark
brows were a straight line above his eyes. She
looked away, aware that she was drawn by his
good looks, and annoyed with herself because of
it, and made no further attempt to talk for the rest

of their journey. Instead she occupied herself with trying to remember the prices of the various things she had seen, changing the guldens into pounds and back again and getting very muddled. Her thoughts ran on, seeking ways of being economical; a sewing machine would be a great help; she would be able to make some of her own clothes then; perhaps there was one somewhere in the house—there was still the big cupboard under the stairs to turn out.

Her companion stopped before her door and got out to open it for her and hand her her basket, a courtesy she hadn't looked for. If she hadn't been so sure that he would snub her, she would have asked him in for a cup of tea; as it was she thanked him for her lift very nicely and asked how she might get Charlie when she wanted him.

'Turn right at the gates,' he told her, 'follow the drive round to the back of the castle, the garages are there. Go in and out as you please, if there is no one about, the doors are only locked at night.' He turned to go, but at the door he paused. 'Your business was satisfactory?'

'Yes, thanks.' She was longing to tell someone about it; that she would be able to live in this dear little house for months, that there was more money than she had expected. Instead she stood silent, waiting for him to go, trying not to notice the way he was staring at her. At length he said: 'The *dominee* will be coming to visit you within the next day or two, his name is Rietveld, he speaks English. His daughter will probably come with him. She has just finished her studies at High School, her name is Loes.'

Something in his voice aroused her curiosity. Loes—a pretty name and probably a pretty girl in whom he was interested, perhaps more than interested; the idea dispirited her. She thanked him for the information in a level voice and added a polite 'good evening'. She was, she warned herself, standing behind the closed door listening to the almost soundless departure of the Rolls, getting a little too interested in him herself, and that would be a foolish thing to do, since he disliked her. She sighed and went to put on the kettle; a cup of tea was supposed to cure most things; perhaps it would cure the peculiar sense of loneliness she was feeling.

a poor humble soul for herself all week—could not
hurt much, she wondered.

CHAPTER THREE

HER visitors called the next day, just as she was
settling down to an afternoon of knitting and reading. She had had a busy morning turning out the
cupboard under the stairs and she had found a
sewing machine—an out-of-date German model,
which, as far as she could see, was still functioning
perfectly. Its discovery set her head buzzing with
plans to make new curtains for the bedrooms and
loose covers for the chairs; there was, she was discovering happily, a great deal to do. She had expected to miss her busy hospital life and her
friends, and perhaps she did miss them a little, but
there was no time to sit and mope—her days, she
could see, were going to be well filled.

Dominee Rietveld looked rather nice, tall and
thin and stooping, with a kind face and an absentminded manner. The girl with him was just as Henrietta had guessed; pretty small, and inclined to
plumpness with big china blue eyes and a quantity
of fair hair hanging around her shoulders. Henrietta
disliked her on sight; she didn't like her mouth—
it had a selfish pout, and the blue eyes were sly
despite the charming smile. She invited her guests
in, installed them in the velvet chairs and drew up

a more humble seat for herself. Mr van Hessel had been right, the *dominee* spoke very good English, and Loes spoke it well enough, making rather a fuss about pronunciation and taking care that she was the focal point of the conversation. His wife, Mijnheer Rietveld explained, had died some ten years previously; he depended on the company of his devoted daughter as well as on her housewifery. 'So young,' he pointed out gently, 'to carry the heavy responsibility of a household, and it is such a waste for a pretty girl to have to remain at home here with her old father.'

Henrietta murmured politely. It wasn't a waste for Loes, not while Mr van Hessel was on the point of melting under those blue eyes. I'd like to see her in action, she thought, and asked how old her younger visitor might be.

'Almost nineteen,' Loes told her, and added unforgivably: 'And you? You are much older, I think?'

'Oh, much.' Henrietta smiled a little and added naughtily: 'You don't need to fear competition from me, you know.' She got up. 'You'll have a cup of tea? I'll just put the kettle on.'

When she got back to her chair Loes asked with a puzzled air: 'You said competition—why is that?'

Henrietta put her lovely head on one side. 'I rather gathered that Mr van Hessel was an admirer of yours. I expect you have been hoping that I was cross-eyed or middle-aged, haven't you?'

The *dominee* laughed at what he understood to be a delightful little joke, and Loes laughed too, only her blue eyes had become hard and her mouth peevish. 'We are friends,' she said crossly, and when Henrietta got up to make the tea she followed her into the kitchen. 'I do not wish to say this before Papa,' she explained distantly, 'but I think that Marnix van Hessel is in love with me—well, almost.'

'Bully for you,' Henrietta's voice was dry. 'And you—are you in love with him?'

Loes shrugged her shoulders. 'I am very young and he is more than forty years old'—she made it sound like a hundred—'but I should like to live at the castle.' She became all at once plaintive. 'His mother does not like me.'

'Oh, has he got a mother?' asked Henrietta with interest. Somehow Mr van Hessel didn't seem human enough to be anyone's son, but of course that was nonsense.

Loes nodded. 'Naturally he has a mother, but of course she will not live for ever.'

'That's a beastly thing to say!' said Henrietta sharply. 'You should be ashamed of yourself.' She picked up the tea tray and went back to the *dominee*, who smiled vaguely at them both, doubtless thinking how nice it was that they had become

friends so quickly; it emboldened him to invite
Henrietta to attend church on Sunday, and suggest
that Loes should call for her and then sit with her
so that she might be guided through the service.
She accepted gracefully because he was a dear old
thing, blandly ignoring Loes's sulky face.

They took their leave shortly after that, and Henrietta went back to her knitting, her thoughts as
busy as her needles. Of course she didn't much
care for Mr van Hessel, she reminded herself, but
she was loath to see him trapped into marrying that
conceited chit of a girl—spoilt, rude and unkind.
They would make a fine pair, but then she frowned,
because that wasn't true; Mr van Hessel was high-
handed and bad-tempered, but his manners were
nice when he chose; she hadn't forgotten his grave
courtesy in the shop that first morning, and he had
made her purchases for her and arranged for her to
have help—and he had seen about Charlie too, and
then only yesterday he had—and not from choice,
she felt sure—driven her to Tilburg and back,
whereas someone else might have shrugged their
shoulders and left her to chance her luck on her
own or not go. Her frown deepened; his kindnesses
had grown into quite a formidable list; he couldn't
be nearly as bad as she had thought him to be,
perhaps it was just his unfortunate manner; she decided then and there to keep her temper in future,
however much he annoyed her.

She had had her supper and was sitting cosily by the stove when the front door knocker was thumped with a good deal of force. She glanced at the clock; it was a little late for a visit, but all the same she went to see who it was: Mr van Hessel, quite blocking her view of the street behind him.

'Oh, hullo,' she exclaimed, and felt a surge of pleasure at the sight of him despite the shortcomings of his character.

He never seemed to say hullo or good morning; now he snapped: 'Never open your door without asking who is outside. It should be kept shut...'

She started to close it. 'Well, all right,' she said sweetly, 'if you want it that way.'

A large and beautifully polished shoe prevented her from moving it another inch. 'Do not mock me, my good girl,' he cautioned her, 'I do not care for it.'

'No, I daresay not,' she agreed cheerfully, her pretty head half round the door. 'I don't suppose anyone in the village would dare, would they? Only not being one of them I don't feel intimidated. And now will you come in, or are you going off in a huff?'

He threw back his head and let out a great roar of laughter. 'I will come in, if I may, Miss Brodie.'

She held the door wide and led the way through to the sitting room, and he stopped in the doorway to exclaim: 'There are no flowers—your aunt had them.'

'Possibly,' said Henrietta dryly. 'I looked in the florists' in Tilburg, but really, the prices at this time of year...' She bit her lip because now he might wonder if she had any money, enough to live on, that was. She rushed on: 'I bought some seeds, so as soon as the weather gets better I shall start a garden. I know it's very small at the back, but at least I shall be able to pick flowers every day if I should wish to.' She waved a large, well-shaped hand towards one of the velvet chairs. 'Sit down, do, but take off that jacket first—it's warm in here.' She smiled at him and got no response. 'Is it about the ground rent?'

He was still standing, his face serious, although she had that nasty feeling again that he was amused about something. 'No,' he said finally, 'not this time, and before I take off my jacket I have something for you.'

He slid a careful hand inside the heavy sheepskin and brought out a very small black kitten with saucer eyes and enormous ears, and held it out to her.

'For me? Really for me to keep? But how kind, and how did you guess...?' She had the scrap of black fur cupped in her hands, smiling across at him. 'He makes it perfect,' she declared. 'Is he from your home?'

'Yes—the mother had only two kittens and we have kept the other.'

She searched his face, feeling puzzled. 'It was so kind of you to think of me,' she told him again.

He smiled. 'You will now have to stay here, will you not?'

'Oh, but I wanted to,' she assured him. 'I shall be able to live here for several months, perhaps much longer, I'm not quite sure...' She stopped, for she had actually been on the point of telling him about the legacy. To cover her discomfiture she took the tea cosy off the table by her chair, turned it upside down and sat the kitten carefully in it before setting it before the stove. The small creature went to sleep at once and she asked: 'Would you like a cup of coffee—I was going to make one.'

'Thank you. Miss Brodie, it is only fair to tell you that I helped your aunt draw up her will, and I know to a cent how much money she left you. Is that all you have?'

His voice was different now; kind and friendly and quite uncurious. She heard herself saying: 'No, not quite; I have a little money I've saved and of course there's my super-an., but I can't get at that until I retire or marry.'

'You will have enough for six months?'

'I think so. I'm not extravagant and I've enough

clothes—I like having new things, but I can manage without, and I don't eat a great deal.'

He wasn't looking at her. 'There is always the possibility of some kind of job later on if you should wish to stay.'

'Yes, but I should have to get a work permit and I don't know if that's easy.'

'Quite simple. If you should need advice or help I hope that you will come to me.' He frowned suddenly and said almost angrily: 'I was fond of your aunt.'

So that was why he was being kind! Henrietta stifled a disappointment she didn't understand and went to make the coffee. Back in the sitting room again, she said: 'I had my visitors this afternoon—you were quite right, Loes Rietveld is a very pretty girl.'

She found herself watching his face and its expression baffled her.

'Isn't she? And extremely capable for her age. She runs her father's house most expertly, and besides that, she is remarkably accomplished.'

And you can say that again! thought Henrietta; he had accused her of mocking him not half an hour since, and yet he hadn't seen the mockery in the horrid girl's blue eyes, and that mockery would get worse if he married her. She would lead him a wretched life, she wasn't his kind of girl; he needed someone who would love him so much that

whatever hurt he had suffered in the past would be
gone for good—that there had been a hurt she felt
sure; his ill-humour and cold manner were only a
cover-up of his true nature, a shield against the
same thing happening again. He must have been
very young...

'Why do you look at me in that way?' he demanded so sharply that she almost dropped her
cup.

'We must think of a name for the kitten,' she
smiled.

'We, Miss Brodie? He is yours, not ours.'

Very rude, thought Henrietta, and then: poor
lamb. Out loud she said brightly: 'He shall be
Henry...' and to her surprise he answered at once:
'Oh, yes—Henry the Fourth, is it not—"I had
rather be a kitten and cry mew."'

'Yes.'

'It also goes very well with Henrietta.'

'Yes—I hadn't thought of that.'

'You are a surprising young woman, Miss Brodie.' He put down his cup. 'I will go and leave you
to become better acquainted with Henry. Do not
come to the door, it is a cold night.'

He had pulled on his jacket as he spoke and had
gone before her cheerful 'good night' had had a
chance to be delivered.

She didn't see him at all for two days, and then
it was on the Sunday. Church was at ten o'clock,

and if Loes did as her father had suggested she
would be called for. She did her small chores, put
on her only hat, a felt whose very plainness served
to make her pretty face even prettier, left her coat
and gloves handy, and went to sit by the stove with
Henry on her lap. He had taken kindly to her, and
showed no wish to go further than the back garden,
and at night had already installed himself on the
end of her bed, climbing up the counterpane to find
the warm patch over the hot water bottle. Henrietta
sat tickling his small chin, thinking about the two
days which had passed.

They had been pleasant; she had explored the
village on foot, every small lane of it, she had visited the churches, the Catholic at the other end of
the village, the Protestant close by, an austere
whitewashed building with a tiled steeple, six-
teenth-century, with its plain glass windows and
rather bare interior. But the pews were beautifully
carved and there were quantities of memorials on
its walls, most of them for dead and gone van Hessels; they must have lived in Gijzelmortel for hun-
dreds of years. She had discovered the *dominee*'s
home too, a square, flat-faced house close to the
church, the only large house in the whole village
save for the castle. The one place she hadn't poked
her charming nose into was the garage where Charlie was housed. She had avoided the big gates as
far as possible, but she had made up her mind that

on Tuesday she would take the little car into Tilburg for the day. The weather was still cold and the roads were icy, but once she was on the motorway she would be all right, and now that she had been along the lane from the village in the daylight, she saw nothing there to frighten her.

She put Henry into his tea cosy as the knocker sounded; so Loes had decided to come. Henrietta went to open the door and they made polite conversation while she put on her coat and gloves and fetched her handbag. Loes looked very pretty; Henrietta had formed that lightning opinion at the first glance. A powder blue coat with a fur collar and a little blue cap—very fetching, and it put her unassuming tweeds quite in the shade. Not that that mattered; there was no one to see. She corrected herself; there was—Mr van Hessel; since so many of his ancestors lay buried in the little church, then it must be assumed that he was also one of its pillars.

The two girls spoke little on the way to church, and then in the falsely bright voices of two women who didn't like each other, and Loes's face was peevish, but at the church entrance this disappeared, to be replaced by a look of such sweetness that Henrietta could only stare as she was shepherded up the aisle with all the care of a hen with one chick and urged into a front seat just below the pulpit. Though not before she had had the time to see Mr van Hessel on the other side of the aisle, sitting in a front pew too, only his had a large shaped end with the family coat of arms carved upon it. There was someone with him too; an elderly lady, sweet-faced and short and plump, wrapped in a mink coat and with a toque of the same fur on her elegantly dressed hair. Mother, said Henrietta silently, and allowed herself to be edged into a seat on the further side of Loes, so that unless she leaned forward in a conspicuous way or tilted dangerously backwards, she could see nothing of Mr van Hessel—nor could he see her; at least, only the top of her head above her companion's eye-catching cap.

She puzzled her way through the service because Loes was no help at all, so that she stood up in the wrong places and sat down when she shouldn't have, and each time the girl made a show of helping her without doing anything at all to guide her. Henrietta sat, her head tilted back so that she might see the *dominee* several feet above them in the pulpit, and allowed his pleasant voice to argue and cajole over it. Not a word did she understand, naturally, although it seemed to her that the congregation was being taken to task over something or other.

She began to ruminate on her groceries for the week to come, and whether she could afford to have both lunch and tea in Tilburg. She was still doing little sums in her head when the sermon ended, the last hymn was sung and the congregation prepared to go, and by a fortunate chance someone came up to engage Loes in a low-voiced conversation, so that Henrietta, taking no notice of her restraining hand, edged past and started on her way out.

Mr van Hessel was only a yard or so from her, coming from his own pew. His cold gaze barely acknowledged her as he stood aside for his mother to precede him, but the little lady gave her a bright look and smiled; Henrietta had the impression that she would have liked to have stopped and spoken to her, but her son was plainly waiting for her to join him. It amused Henrietta to see how the congregation made way for them, rather as though they had been royalty. She lost sight of them then and waiting only to bid Loes good-bye and thank her for accompanying her to church, she left the church herself. As she reached the square it was to see the Rolls' stately back disappearing through the castle gates. Very feudal, she decided, and went home to Henry.

There were letters for her on Monday morning, from her friends at hospital and Mr Boggett; a dry-as-dust document hoping that she had found everything in good order and he was hers to command. Henrietta swept and polished and cooked her solitary meal and contentedly answered her post. A day had never gone so quickly, and as she got ready for bed that night, the uneasy idea that perhaps she was becoming that old-fashioned creature, a spinster, crossed her mind. Spinsters had cats and lived in little cottages. She dismissed the idea rather doubtfully and concentrated on her plans for the next day, making a list of what she needed to get and adding at the last minute a book from which she might teach herself at least basic Dutch.

The last of the snow had melted by morning and by ten o'clock she was ready to leave and go in search of Charlie. The circular drive round the castle was larger than she had supposed. She followed it almost to the back of the old building and found the garage easily enough——a large rambling row of outhouses, expertly converted, with several garages and dwellings above them. Someone had cleaned her little car; it shone with polish, and when she looked at the petrol gauge, she found that the tank was full too. There was no one to be seen as she backed out and drove back to the gates and through the village, on to the country road which would take her to the motorway. She had been a little nervous to begin with, but Charlie was running sweetly and although it was a dull grey day, at least it was neither raining nor snowing. She parked in Tilburg without difficulty and set out to enjoy herself. It was growing dark when she left the town;

she had had her lunch in the same café again and at the end of her afternoon had had tea in one of the smarter restaurants; it had been expensive but worth it, and she travelled home, well content.

There were lights shining from the castle windows as she drove through the gates, and lights over the garages. She stopped and looked around her, then got out of the car to open the garage door, and this time Jan came out of a small door at the side of the building with a cheerful: 'Hullo, miss' and signalled to her to drive Charlie straight in. Henrietta thanked him, picked up her shopping basket and wished him good night as she started back towards the gates. She was half-way there when she saw a car's lights coming towards her and stood on one side to let it pass—the Rolls with Mr van Hessel at the wheel and Loes beside him, and although he didn't appear to see her, Loes did; she waved and smiled for all the world as though they were the greatest of friends, but Henrietta made no response at all—it was dark anyway. She walked rapidly home, surprised at the strength of her dislike for Loes.

She was hanging the freshly washed net curtains at the front bedroom window the next morning when she saw the Rolls glide to a halt before her door and Mr van Hessel, looking cross, get out and thump the knocker. She flung up the old-fashioned sash to peer down at the top of his head and cry: 'Hang on, I'll be down in a jiffy.'

He looked up at her, unsmiling, and before she closed the window she added: 'Oh, dear, you do look cross!'

He didn't say good morning when she opened the door to him, but then he never did. He followed her into the small sitting room and said without preamble: 'I have instructed my agent, Pieter van der Zande, to call upon you with particulars of the ground rent.'

'Oh, good. When will he be coming?' He looked surprised and Henrietta explained: 'I'm not always home, you know, and it might not be convenient for me. After lunch suits me very well—today or tomorrow.'

After a moment, he nodded. 'Very well. How is Henry?'

'In great form, he's taking a nap. He's made himself quite at home—did my aunt have a cat?'

'Yes—when she died I took the beast to live at the castle. Henry is her kitten.'

How kind he is, Henrietta thought confusedly, and how ill-tempered he looks, just as though he can't bear the sight of me. The unwelcome thought that his initial dislike of her had deepened and was disquieting and hurtful. 'I'm very grateful for him,' she said, 'and thank you for letting me know about Mr van der Zande.'

She held out a hand; she had quickly caught on to the custom of shaking hands with everyone at the oddest time, just as though you were never going to see each other again or hadn't met for days. He took the hand and pulled her towards him quite roughly and bent to kiss her surprised mouth.

'I wanted to do that,' and she wasn't sure if he was talking to her or to himself, for without another word he walked out of the house, leaving her to stare after him.

'Well, I never!' said Henrietta.

She tried not to think about him, but it was no good; his handsome frowning face got between her and whatever she was doing, so that in the end she was forced to wrap up warmly and go for a walk. It was too late to do more than eat a snack lunch when she got back, and, anxious to keep her mind occupied, she went into the kitchen and started a batch of bread. It was a placid occupation and soothing. She had just taken the final loaf from the tin oven she had found to set on top of the gas rings, when someone thumped the knocker. The postman, she supposed idly, her mind on her baking, and went to the door as she was, warm from her work and wearing an apron. It was Mr van Hessel, who, without beating about the bush, said curtly: 'I've come to apologize.' He sniffed the air and added: 'You've been baking bread,' and walked past her into the tiny hall without being invited while she was still wondering which of his remarks to answer. Finally she said: 'Don't apologize, I'm not a silly girl, you know. I've just made a batch of loaves.'

She led the way into the sitting room and stood quietly, waiting for him to speak. He cast off his car coat before he did so. 'I know you're not a silly young girl, but that is no excuse for my behaviour.' His eyes searched her face. 'Do you wish for an explanation?'

'Heavens, no—I've been kissed before.' She smiled at him and he smiled back with an unexpected charm which caught her breath so that for something to say, she asked: 'Would you like a cup of tea?' and was surprised when he said yes, adding that if she was going to cut a loaf, he would like a slice of it.

She brought the tray in by the stove and poured his tea and offered him a thick slice of hot bread, lavishly spread. 'It ought to be butter,' she apologized, 'but you said buy margarine and indeed I don't believe I could afford butter.'

He bit into his slice. 'It's delicious—you are a woman of parts, Miss Brodie.'

She longed to ask him to call her Henrietta, but perhaps if she did he would retreat behind that chilly manner again. Instead she remarked: 'What a pleasant town Tilburg is, and such lovely shops. When the weather gets better I shall go to Breda and Eindhoven and explore.' She bent to give Henry a saucer of milk.

'You must let me know when you decide to go; I visit both places twice a week.'

'Oh, do you? Have you got a...' She stopped herself in time; it would never do to ask if he worked.

'Job? Yes, I have,' he had taken her up smoothly. 'I'm a surgeon. I work principally in Eindhoven and Breda and once a week I have a list in Tilburg. Occasionally I go to Leiden or Amsterdam, sometimes to London.'

She poured him more tea. 'So that's why you know St Clement's. You don't have a surgery here? You would be a consultant, of course.'

He smiled faintly. 'Yes—my rooms are in Tilburg, otherwise I travel to consultations.'

'What do you specialize in?'

'Abdominal surgery—alimentary tract, mostly CA.'

'You've been operating today?'

'Yes, at Eindhoven. You're interested in surgery?' He helped himself to a second slice in an absentminded manner.

'Yes, I am, rather, though I've had a medical ward for five years. You see, it was the first vacancy for a Sister's post and I took it. I suppose I thought that I could transfer back to surgical, but I've never had the chance since then.'

He began to tell her about his day, sitting back at his ease by the stove, and when Henry climbed on to his knee, he put out a gentle hand and scratched the little creature's ear with a long blunt finger, smiling down at the kitten. The silver in his dark hair made him even better looking than he was. He was quite different this evening and she wondered if he was allowing her to see what he was really like. Had he discarded his impassive mask just for half an hour or so, so that she might get to know his real self, and if so, would he resume it again? Perhaps he had thought that she was on the lookout for a husband and had kept her at a distance until he was sure that she had designs on him. Well, she had made that fact obvious enough, surely, and her behaviour had been exemplary—well, for most of the time, anyway, save for a few sharp words—the mature, level-headed bachelor girl. He had completed that picture by giving her Henry; probably he knew that bachelor girls turned quickly enough into spinsters with cats for company—like Aunt Henrietta, but at least she had been loved, and that must have been wonderful, even though it was sad to think of all those years…

'What are you thinking about?' asked Mr van Hessel suddenly in a quiet voice.

'Aunt Henrietta.'

'A charming woman, much loved and greatly

respected. Her heart was broken when my uncle died.'

Just as mine would, she thought, just as it will when he marries Loes, but shall I have the courage to go on living here, just to be near him, even though he didn't care two sticks for me? She had never known until that moment how unnerving it was to discover that you loved someone; it was suddenly and blindingly apparent to her that she had done exactly as her aunt had done, only unlike his uncle, Mr van Hessel didn't share her feelings. I must be mad, she mused. I've only known him such a short time and here I am in love with a man who doesn't even look at me. She put her cup down and looked away from him because, as if to contradict her thought, he was staring at her so.

'Have you a dog?' she asked, because it was the first thing which came into her head and she had to break the silence.

'A labrador, Willy, and my mother has a corgi, called Muff. We have a Siamese cat called Thor and Henry's mother, Nolly.'

She was stupidly unable to think of any reply so that he smiled faintly and asked: 'You play the piano?'

'Yes. Not well, though, and I haven't practised for years, but I found some music—I found a sewing machine too, so useful.' She was babbling, and the discovery of a sewing machine could be of no interest to him, but it seemed it was, or he was being polite.

'You make your own clothes?'

'Some of them.'

'A woman of parts.' He put Henry back into his tea cosy and rose to his feet. 'The bread was delicious, Miss Brodie—it is to be hoped that your wifely talents won't be wasted.'

An unanswerable remark. She said snappily: 'Pray don't concern yourself about me, Mr van Hessel,' and saw him to the door where she bade him good night with chilly politeness; a transitory mood which dissolved in no time at all into tears.

CHAPTER FOUR

HENRIETTA slept badly, for Mr van Hessel's handsome features seemed indelibly pictured in her mind, and in the morning he came between everything she tried to do, so that in the end she gave up, put on her outdoor things and went in search of Charlie. It was no day for a drive, but at least it might clear her head and allow her to think of something else. It was still early afternoon and she would go to Breda, she decided, with a defiant look at the grey sky; it was only fifteen miles or so and when she got there she would take herself out to tea.

She hurried through the gates and made her way in the teeth of a nasty wind to the garages. Jan was there, pottering round an elderly and well kept Daimler, and she stopped to talk to him, their conversation a little long-winded, for his English was poor, and although she had taught herself a number of useful phrases, her pronunciation was faulty so that there was a good deal of repetition. They were bringing their little chat to a friendly conclusion when she noticed that the door in the castle wall opposite the narrow footbridge over the moat had opened and a woman was coming towards them.

She spoke to Jan as she joined them, smiled at Henrietta and handed her a note which she opened with some curiosity. Surely Mr van Hessel…

It was from his mother: would she, if she had nothing better to do, care to join the writer for an hour and perhaps stay for a cup of tea?

A spot of cold rain fell on to the paper in her hand; a sign from heaven, she told herself, and nodded at the woman, reinforcing her nod with a '*Ja,*' and adding '*Wanneer?*' and basked in the encouraging smiles of her companions. It was Jan who said: 'Now, miss. This is Klara, the housekeeper, you go with her.'

Henrietta followed the other woman across the moat, pausing in the middle of the bridge to look down at the dark water it spanned. The door was narrow and arched and opened into a narrow passage with plain white plastered walls, its flagstones almost covered by a rich burgundy red carpet. It wasn't very long; the closed door at its end opened into what Henrietta judged to be the main hall of the castle, a circular apartment with a black and white marble floor with a many-coloured carpet covering its centre and a stone staircase curling up the plastered wall at one side, to end in a gallery above them. Very impressive, she found it, but curiously homely too, for there were a great many flowers, exquisitely arranged, and the brass wall sconces had cheerful wine red shades. There was a wide stone fireplace at the back of the hall and on either side of it arched doors, but her guide led her straight across the hall to a door on its further side, knocked, and ushered her in with another smile.

It was a small room considering the size of the castle, with panelled walls, painted white, and a beamed ceiling. A periwinkle blue carpet covered its floor and in the summer it would get all the sun through its narrow windows; now it was pleasantly lighted by a number of lamps in various shades of cream and pale yellow which shone upon the blue covers of the chairs on each side of the fireplace, the large sofa between them and the lovely satin-wood table behind it. There were display cabinets against the walls filled with a wealth of china and silver. Henrietta found it a delightful room and exactly right for its occupant. Mr van Hessel's mother was still a pretty woman, made prettier by the sweetness of her expression. She came across the room with her hand outstretched, saying in a charming voice: 'You will forgive me, I hope—I have been wanting to call upon you, but Marnix said that it would be better to wait until you had settled in, but when I saw you just now from the window, it seemed an excellent opportunity to make your acquaintance.'

She led the way to the fire. 'Please sit, my dear.' She sat herself down opposite Henrietta and studied her without haste. 'You are not in the least like your aunt, at least not in your appearance; you are a very pretty girl—a great deal prettier than Loes Rietveld.' She accompanied this astonishing remark with a satisfied nod and smiled at Henrietta, who smiled back, uncertain what to say. Mr van Hessel's mother had grey eyes like her son, and despite her prettiness, a firm mouth and chin. It seemed more than likely, thought Henrietta shrewdly, that he didn't get his own way with her, at least, not all the time.

'And now tell me all about yourself—I was full of curiosity to see you, naturally, but all Marnix would tell me when I asked him about you was that you weren't in the least like your aunt, and in church it was a little difficult to take a good look at you, so if you do not find me too inquisitive, I should very much like to know something of you. You are, I hear, alone and without family?'

Henrietta answered that question and a dozen more besides, and presently a young girl brought in the tea tray, with a corgi and two cats in her wake. 'They come every afternoon,' explained her hostess, 'for their tea, you know, but not Willy, of course. If he isn't with Marnix he remains aloof until he comes home.'

She poured tea from a small silver teapot, her pleasant voice rambling on about this and that, but not, Henrietta noted with regret, about her son. He wasn't mentioned again and presently she took her leave, but not before she had invited her hostess rather diffidently to visit her one day. 'I don't know if you knew my aunt well?' she asked.

'We were—how do you say?—bosom friends; I had the highest regard for her, my dear. I should very much like to visit you, may I come any day? or perhaps I could send you a message first?'

'That would be fine, and thank you for my delightful afternoon, Mevrouw van Hessel.'

Her companion pulled on an embroidered bell rope by the fireplace and Klara answered it. She led Henrietta across the hall, this time to the great front door, and opened it and then stood there, with it still open, until she was across the bridge and by the gates, she turned as she reached them and watched it being closed, shutting out the lights from within the castle. She sighed; she doubted if she would go to the castle again. She had been, as it were, interviewed, but she doubted if anything further would come of it. There had been a firm basis for Mevrouw van Hessel's friendship with Aunt Henrietta, for they had been of a similar age, but in her own case she could see no real reason for Mr van Hessel's mother wishing to further their acquaintance.

She opened her own front door and went through to the sitting room. Castles and fine furniture were all very well to visit and admire, but she must never forget to be grateful for her own tiny home. It had everything, she told herself stoutly, even dear little Henry, waiting for her in his tea cosy.

Mr van Hessel's agent came the following afternoon, a man of much the same age as Henrietta herself, with fair hair and blue eyes and a serious face. He carried a briefcase in one hand and held a long wicker basket carefully under the other arm.

'Miss Brodie? You expect me, I think.'

'Yes—you're van der Zande, aren't you? Do come in, won't you, and take off your coat.'

He followed her into the sitting room, still holding the basket. The briefcase he put on the table, but the basket he handed to her. 'Jonkheer van Hessel sends you flowers from his greenhouses, he hopes that you will like them.'

There were tulips and narcissi, daffodils and violets. She examined them with delight, wondering if Mr van Hessel had chosen them himself. 'How very kind!' she exclaimed. 'If I write a little note presently would you be kind enough to deliver it for me? They're exquisite!'

Mr van der Zande beamed at her. 'You like them? I did not know which flowers to choose, but I am glad then you are pleased with them.'

So Mr van Hessel hadn't chosen them himself— it had been foolish of her to suppose that he might.

She remembered something else. 'What did you call him?' She frowned. 'Mr van Hessel, I mean.'

'He is not a mister, Miss Brodie, he is a *jonkheer*—that is a title in our country. His father and uncle were that also, it was from his uncle that he inherited the castle—family, you see. It is perhaps a little difficult to explain; our *adel* is not quite as yours.'

'Well, I wouldn't know, but he might have told me—here have I been calling him Mister all the time. And his mother, what should I have called her?'

'She is a *jonkvrouwe,* Miss Brodie, but it is permissible to call her Mevrouw, but when she is spoken of it is correct that she be called Mevrouw de Douairiere.' He took no notice of Henrietta's 'Well, I never!' but went on earnestly: 'Jonkheer van Hessel is also a surgeon, so it's not too grave a fault that you should address him as Mister.'

She stared at him, wondering if he was as serious as he looked; apparently he was—a nice young man without a sense of humour. 'Oh, I must remember,' she told him gravely, anxious not to upset him; it was all so important to him, she could see that. 'How fortunate that you mentioned it.' She smiled at his sober face. 'Would you like a cup of tea now; or later?'

'The work first,' he declared firmly, so she sat down in one of the red velvet chairs and waved

him to the other, rather liking him despite his so-
berness, and watched him take a number of papers
out of his case, prepared to give him her full attention.

The business was simple enough once he had
explained it to her, handing her the documents so
that she might see them for herself. They were
some three hundred years old, the original deeds
of gift, written in a spidery script, and naturally
enough in Dutch, and old Dutch at that. Henrietta
examined them with interest, but when he offered
to translate them for her she assured him that was
quite unnecessary; she had no reason to suspect
Jonkheer van Hessel's integrity—a remark which
brought a look of horror into her companion's face,
so that she felt compelled to apologize when he
said sternly: 'The Jonkheer is a man of the highest
reputation, he would not take a cent which was not
his.'

'Oh, I'm sure you're right, perhaps I put it rather
badly, what I mean is: I trust him absolutely, so
that there is no need for me to know any more. I'll
just pay what I have to.'

Mijnheer van der Zande looked mollified and
handed her another paper containing a long list of
names with hers at the end. 'This is the original
record; when the houses were first built and given
as life gifts to those whom Jonkheer van Hessel's
ancestor considered worthy, their names were en-

tered here, and ever since that time, whenever a house has changed hands, the name of the new occupant is entered upon it.'

'I feel like a piece of history in the making,' she remarked, then saw that he hadn't understood her. 'How much do I have to pay?'

'Ten gulden a year, Miss Brodie.'

'Ten gulden?—but that's ridiculous! It must cost thousands to keep these places in such good order, and they're modernized too.'

'The Jonkheer considers it his duty to do this— he is a rich man, but even if he were not, I am quite sure that he would continue to do as his ancestors have done.'

Whatever else he was, mused Henrietta, Marnix van Hessel inspired respect and loyalty in his agent—probably in everyone who worked for him too; that he inspired a quite different feeling in herself, she chose to ignore. She fetched a ten-gulden note and waited while Mijnheer van der Zande wrote out a receipt in a neat copperplate hand, then went to get the tea.

He relaxed then, and it was over the tea cups that he confided to her that he wished to marry a young lady called Engelina, who from all accounts was small and young and timid, aspects of her nature which seemed to delight him. It was unfortunate, he told Henrietta, that he was possessed of a strong-minded mother who refused to consider her as a daughter-in-law.

'But surely,' expostulated Henrietta, 'you can please yourself? How old are you? Twenty-five? Well, twenty-six—a grown man who can choose whom he wishes to marry. Have you brothers or sisters?'

'A sister—a schoolteacher in Dordrecht.'

'Could your mother not go and live with her if she doesn't like to live alone, then you could marry your Engelina. Do you live in the village?'

'Yes—at least, I have the tenancy of a house behind the castle, it goes with my work, you understand. It is a nice house and I would not wish to leave the Jonkheer's service.'

'But why should you? I should think he was completely satisfied with you and would want you to stay for ever. No, you must marry your Engelina and persuade your mother that she is mistaken in her opinion.'

He threw her a grateful look. 'You are very kind, Miss Brodie, and your advice is good—I would like to come and see you again and talk to you. You see, I cannot talk to Engelina, for she lives in Eindhoven and we see each other very seldom.'

'But why? Surely you get plenty of free time?'

'Of course, but my mother enjoys my company.'

Henrietta bit back what she would have liked to say about his mother; she said gently: 'Look, you must be firm. You're living your life, not hers, you know. Go and see your girl whenever you want to and then your mother will know that you're in earnest. It might be a bit unpleasant at first, but she'll come round.'

He brightened. 'Perhaps if you will visit my mother?'

'With pleasure. Now will you wait a minute and I'll write a note to Mr—no, Jonkheer van Hessel.'

She composed a stiff little note of thanks and addressed it correctly in her large firm handwriting, and gave it to Mijnheer van der Zande to take with him, speeding him on his way with a few more encouraging words, for it seemed to her that, nice though he was, he needed a good deal of bolstering up.

After she had closed the door behind him she spent a happy hour arranging her flowers, talking to Henry while she did so, and then because she felt a trifle lonely, she got out the music she had found and spent the rest of the evening at the piano, playing Chopin with a good deal of feeling; his romantic style suited her mood.

The best part of a week went by, each day filled with housework, cooking, hours at the piano and even more hours ploughing through her self-taught Dutch lessons, and when she got bored or tired of being indoors, she went for long walks. She had gone to church again too, this time sitting at the back, where she had a splendid view of Jonkheer van Hessel's vast frame from the back and a much more annoying view of Loes casting what could only be described as languishing glances in his direction. She had whipped out of the church door as quickly as she could at the end of the service, but not so fast that he had the time to turn deliberately in his pew and scan the congregation. Counting heads, she told herself flippantly as she slipped across the aisle in order to escape the first outgoing surge of people. He had seen her, she knew, but no smile had crossed his face, and she had pretended not to have seen him.

The weather had changed; the grey skies had given way to a pale, chilly blue and there was sunshine, though quite without warmth, for part of each day so that the icy roads never quite thawed. No weather to take out the car, but she had become a little restless, owing, she refused to admit, to the fact that she hadn't seen anything of Marnix van Hessel for several days.

She fetched Charlie just before midday when everyone else was indoors at their dinner; a few hours in Tilburg would do her good. She drove carefully along the treacherous road and was thankful to reach the motorway and drive the rest of the way in comparative peace of mind, aware at the back of her mind that she had been a fool to attempt the journey in the first place. But she forgot the hazards of driving Charlie on icy roads once she got to the shops; she enjoyed herself and stayed longer than she had intended so that it was already dark when she eventually turned the little car's nose towards home. It wasn't at all bad on the motorway, but once on the narrow side road to Gijzelmortel, she wished again that she had never undertaken the trip, for with the dark the frost had returned and the road had become a nasty mixture of rough, uneven surface and patches of skating rink ice.

It was on one of these, while she was still several kilometres from the village, that Charlie went into a skid. Henrietta was quite a good driver and not the panicky type. She had had skids before, but always on a road wide enough to manoeuvre the car, but now there was no room at all. Charlie, spinning gaily and quite unmanageable, ended up at a sharp angle on the steep slope of grass which bordered the road on either side, and beyond them were narrow canals, iced over... Henrietta climbed out, muttering nastily under her breath. It was very dark by now and she had forgotten her torch. It was to be hoped that someone would come along the road sooner or later, but in the meantime it was extremely cold. She could get back into the car, but anyone passing might suppose that Charlie had merely been abandoned and drive on without stopping.

She stood for a few chilly minutes, her hand on the tilted bonnet, and then, her eyes accustomed to the gloom, got back on to the road. Its surface precluded any form of exercise, so slippery was it, so she contented herself with stamping her feet and clapping her hands, hoping that someone would come soon, for little Henry would be wanting his supper—besides, when she thought about it, the village seemed a long way away, standing there in the dark cold. She shivered and renewed her stamping and clapping, then remembered that when she had fetched the milk that morning she had overheard someone in the shop say that Jonkheer van Hessel would be going to Eindhoven that day, which meant that there was little chance of him returning home along the side road—not, she told herself stoutly, that it mattered at all, anyone would do, only she would have liked to have seen him. He would have been reassuring in the dark. And also, she reminded herself, he would have probably made a number of caustic remarks; at least she was spared that.

She was spared nothing; she saw the car's headlights some way off and recognized the restrained purr of the engine. The Rolls' powerful lamps picked out poor Charlie leaning drunkenly in the ditch, and herself standing by the roadside. Marnix van Hessel wasted no time in unnecessary questions, nor, for that matter, did he show any signs of sympathy, let alone utter any of the conventional words of concern.

'Only a fool would take out a car like Charlie in weather like this,' he observed bitingly.

Her delight and relief at seeing him turned instantly into a fine rage. 'You horrible man!' she blazed. 'That's a fine thing to say—I'm half dead with cold and it's—it's dark...'

He laughed. 'What, no torch? My dear good woman—oh, forgive me, my dear Miss Brodie, a torch is quite essential when you go driving, especially when you are alone and after dark. And you will forgive me if I say that your voice sounds to me as though you are very much alive and decidedly cross.'

He went over to her car and gave it a cursory inspection. 'Charlie will have to stay here for the night, I'm afraid. Get into my car, Miss Brodie, I will take you home.'

'No,' said Henrietta, 'I won't. If you would be good enough to ask someone in the village to fetch me, or better still, get Charlie back on to the road, then I need trouble you no further.'

'What a nasty stubborn temper.' His voice was silky. 'You'll do as I say, Miss Brodie.'

He swept her up carelessly as he spoke and dumped her in the Rolls, rather in the manner of a man lifting a troublesome child out of the way, and then got in beside her, fastened her seat belt for her and sent the car slowly into the dark night ahead of them. He didn't say a word on the short journey, and she was too busy fighting tears and clenching her teeth together to stop them from chattering, to speak.

He brought the Rolls to a precise halt outside her front door. 'The key?' he asked, and when her cold hands fumbled at her handbag, he took it from her and opened it. 'It's in the front pocket,' she told him peevishly, and he took it with a polite 'May I?' and went to open the door. She was already getting out when he came back to help her over the glassy cobbles, and once inside, he walked her into the dining-room, took off her coat and gloves, cast her fur bonnet aside and said:

'Now go upstairs and undress and take a shower. I'll make some tea.'

A hot shower and tea sounded like heaven, but: 'I'll manage very well, thank you, Jonkheer van Hessel. I'm obliged to you for bringing me home.' She paused to allow her teeth to have a good chatter, and when she had them under control again: 'Don't let me keep you.'

'Those are doctor's orders,' he told her blandly, 'and if you have any out-of-date ideas about taking a shower while I'm in the house, you can forget them—I'd do the same for anyone, old, young, plain or pretty, man, woman or child.'

He strode past her impatiently and opened the

stove; as she climbed the stairs she heard him talking in the pleasantest voice imaginable to Henry.

He was outside fetching in more coal when she went downstairs, and by the time she had showered and emerged, cosily wrapped in her pink quilted dressing gown, her hair hanging damply down her back, he had made the tea and set the tray on one of the little side tables. Henrietta saw, with a sinking heart, that there was only one cup and saucer. 'You'll have a cup?' she asked him in quite a timid voice, 'I'm sorry I was so rude and cross.'

He was already making for the door. 'Your various moods are no concern of mine, Miss Brodie, so you do not need to apologize for them, and as I shall be dining at the *dominee*'s house within the hour, I must refuse the tea. Good night.'

The forthright speech, combined with the warmth of the room and the prospect of her tea, had the effect of reviving her drooping spirits so that she said with some heat: 'Well, if you talk like that at the dining table, I doubt if you will ever get asked again—or perhaps the people in the village are used to your rudeness. Well, I'm not! You can be a duke for all I care, but your manners are sadly lacking.' She added blightingly: 'I know of nothing more annoying than being under an obligation to someone you can't stand at any price.' With which parting shot she dismissed him with a cool nod, sat down and picked up the tea pot. 'I shall keep out of your way,' she assured him.

He laughed. 'I had no idea that you had been putting yourself in my way,' he observed blandly. 'Should I be flattered? I must confess that I hadn't noticed... Good night, my good woman, or should it be good-bye?'

He had gone. Henrietta sat with her cooling tea, shedding a few tears and presently feeling a good deal better for this relief to her feelings, she fed Henry and got herself some supper which she didn't eat. He really must dislike her very much, she decided, pushing scrambled egg round and round her plate and giving it finally to the ever hungry kitten, and yet he was always coming to her aid, one way or another, though probably from a sense of duty; she would have to put him out of her mind, and the quicker the better. She would begin that very minute. Fired by this resolution, she cleared away her uneaten supper, then got out her *Hugo's Dutch for Beginners* and studied it until bed-time.

Loes called the next day. Henrietta had just settled down to an afternoon of piano playing when she was interrupted to answer the door. She wasn't expecting anyone; Jan had been that morning to tell her that he had fetched Charlie, made sure that there had been no harm done, and garaged her car once more at the castle, and when she had asked him if he knew of another garage where she might put it, he had looked so worried and upset that she had said no more about it, for he seemed to think that she wasn't satisfied with his care of her car; it took her a good five minutes of tactful talking to convince him.

Loes was looking charming in a coat with a fur-lined hood, and Henrietta, who felt the beginnings of a cold and was wearing a thick sweater and a rather worthy tweed skirt, felt at an instant disadvantage. All the same she invited her visitor in, offered coffee and went into the kitchen to make it, wondering as she did so why Loes should suddenly decide to come and see her. She begged her to remove her coat, poked up the stove and returned to pour the coffee, all the time talking about nothing in particular. They were sitting drinking it, the picture of amiable friendliness, before Loes finally deserted the generalities.

'You play the piano?' she wanted to know.

'A little,' admitted Henrietta cautiously, 'just to amuse myself, you know.' Surely she wasn't going to be roped in to play for Sunday School or its equivalent in Holland?

'How clever,' said Loes with a warmth which wasn't in the least sincere. 'I am not clever, although I believe that I make amusing conversation. Marnix—Jonkheer van Hessel—says that is sufficient, for I am so pretty—at least he thinks so.'

She smiled at Henrietta, who smiled back to hide her outraged feelings at such conceit and said in a voice whose woodenness entirely escaped her listener: 'He must admire you greatly.' She sounded like a character from a Jane Austen novel, but Loes's English was strictly of the school variety.

Loes looked smug and Henrietta had a regrettable itch to slap her.

'Yes. I have made up my mind to marry him—just imagine, to be a *jonkheer*'s wife!' Her blue eyes sparkled and she added spitefully, 'He does not admire dark girls,' she glanced down at her own plumpish form, 'and you are a big girl, too, are you not, Miss Brodie—but perhaps girl is not the right word?' Her voice held innocent inquiry.

'Oh, definitely not. I'm approaching middle age—I am what we call in England an old maid.'

Her visitor gave her a suspicious look and encountered a calm, smiling face. How fortunate, thought Henrietta, sustaining both calm and smile with difficulty, that I learned self-control from an early age. She continued, still smiling: 'As I've already told you, you don't need to fear competition from me.' Her voice was very sweet. 'I'm quite hopeless at toadying to my betters.'

'Toadying? What does that mean?'

'Oh, it's difficult for me to explain in English. Ask Jonkheer van Hessel when you see him again.'

Loes finished her tea and made preparations to

leave. 'I shall see him tomorrow; I am going to the castle to borrow a book which he wishes me to read, I shall certainly ask him then.' She cast a sidelong glance at Henrietta. 'We had a delightful dinner party yesterday. Father suggested that you should be invited, but I didn't think that Marnix would have liked that.'

Henrietta got to her feet too, by now heartily sick of the girl. 'I wouldn't have liked it either,' she declared tartly. 'What a pity that you have to go so soon, but you've achieved your purpose in coming, haven't you?'

Her visitor looked puzzled. 'Achieved? What is that for a word?'

'Oh, I'm no good at explaining,' Henrietta excused herself airily, and swept Loes to the door, where they shook hands in much the same way as a pair of boxers before round one. It was a pleasure to shut the door on the girl; she told Henry so in an angry voice. 'So he doesn't like dark girls? or big ones, either.' She stumped upstairs and took a good look at herself in the bedroom mirror. She was dark, true enough, and big, but her shape was all that any girl would wish for and there wasn't anything wrong with her face. She scowled at her reflection and went downstairs to air her bruised feelings before Henry, who studied her from the warmth of his tea cosy and then climbed out and wobbled across to sit on her knee, his round eyes fixed on her face.

'Well, at least you like me,' she declared, and kissed him soundly.

CHAPTER FIVE

HENRIETTA woke to driving rain the next morning, so cold that it froze as it touched the ground. It was a pleasant thought that she had no need to go out. She fetched coal and wood, set the little stove roaring and got down to a number of jobs which kept her busy enough, so that she lunched late. She had cleared away her snack meal and settled to her canvas work when she was disturbed by the sound of a plane flying low—so low that she went to the front door to have a look. The sky was uniformly dark grey and the icy rain was still teeming down and there was nothing to be seen in the dreary emptiness above her head. She was on the point of going in again when an airliner swooped from behind the houses on the other side of the square, barely missing their gabled roofs, and then swerved away again, gaining height in a sharp turn. The roar of its engines was no longer regular; it was going to crash close to the village, perhaps even nearer than that, on to the crowded little houses on the other side of the bandstand. Henrietta ran back into the sitting room to close down the stove, tugged on her boots and the elderly coat she kept behind the kitchen door, snatched up a scarf and was at the open door when a Citroën estate car slithered to a halt in front of her.

'Go up to the castle,' Marnix van Hessel instructed her in a calm voice she couldn't help but admire, leaning out of the window the better to speak to her. 'That plane's on the point of crashing—get organized to take any casualties. My mother is telephoning the police, by the time you get there she will be ready to help in any way you wish.' He lifted a hand in salute. 'And go carefully, the ground is like glass.'

He was off again, Jan beside him, circling the square to run down one of the narrow lanes on the other side. Henrietta banged the door behind her and, mindful of his warning, started to walk carefully towards the castle gates. She hadn't quite reached them when there was a mighty explosion and a great pall of black smoke billowed into the air beyond the village. Quite forgetting his warning, she began to run.

She was half-way over the bridge when the great door was flung open by Klara. Henrietta flung off her coat and was waved on towards the sitting room where she found Jonkvrouw van Hessel at the telephone. She finished speaking as Henrietta went in and said in a voice as calm as her son's had been: 'Ah, there you are my dear. Tell me what you wish us all to do—there are plenty of us, and there will be more.'

Henrietta's brain was working with steady coolness now; there wasn't much time and she mustn't
forget anything. 'The furniture—all that can be
moved—out of the hall and as many pillows and
blankets brought in as possible, laid in small piles
so that they can be got at easily. A table with a
bowl, soap, towels, a brush and hot water and
someone there to keep it ready for use at any moment. A second table, big enough to lie down on—
cover it with a white sheet—plenty of tea ready.
Are there any motherly women here who could
take charge of the children if there are any—babies
too.' She was in the hall now, and as she talked
Jonkvrouw van Hessel repeated everything she
said in Dutch to the ever-growing group gathered
there. Some of them moved away to get started and
she said urgently: 'We need men at the doors to
help with the carrying. Some of the people are going to look terrible, too—will you tell them all
that? It's very important.' She watched the older
woman speak to the women around them and they
nodded, while some of them detached themselves
and hurried away. They were working fast and
without fuss; the furniture had gone or had been
pushed aside, the table was already there and a
small stream of people were going to and fro with
pillows and blankets.

'Old sheets,' went on Henrietta, her practical
mind taking over once more, 'to tear up if neces-

sary, and broom handles or walking sticks—or umbrellas if there's nothing else—for splints, you know. And on that chest over there as many pairs of scissors as can be found—to cut clothing off, and some bowls in case anyone needs to be sick. I suppose Marnix has some dressings around?' She was quite unconscious that she had called him by his Christian name and she didn't see her companion's quick glance. 'He'll want to fetch those for himself. Now, let's see—cotton wool, for injections—spirit, eau de cologne will do if there's nothing else, warm milk ready in case there are some hungry babies—cups, mugs, paper hankies.' She was ticking off the items on her fingers. 'Safety pins... Has anyone told Dominee Rietveld and Father Karsten?'

The hall had filled up with people who had come from the village with offers of help and someone started off to fetch both men, but they came in together at that moment and Henrietta sighed with relief. 'I daresay I've forgotten a lot, but we've got the basics—now all we have to do is sort everyone out so that none of us get in each other's way.'

Something quickly enough arranged with the help of Jonkvrouw van Hessel and the quiet women around her. Henrietta thought how splendid they were and how fast and hard they had worked. Most of them she knew by sight at least, and it was then that she noticed that Loes wasn't amongst them; she was standing apart, over in a corner, her expression a mixture of excitement and sulkiness, not helping at all. Henrietta was on the point of going over to her when a car screeched to a halt outside and the two stalwart men from the gardens who had been pressed into service flung the door wide and went outside. The Citroën was crammed; that much Henrietta saw as she followed them—children, a dozen of them, some of them unconscious, and those who weren't unnaturally quiet.

Jonkheer van Hessel and Jan were out of their seats almost before he had stopped the car and began unloading their pitiful cargo; the conscious ones first to the two men and other willing helpers who had followed them out, and then, very carefully, the unconscious children. Henrietta took a toddler from Marnix's arms.

'Get them ready for me to examine, will you?' His voice sounded harsh and he cast a quick glance through the open castle door. 'You seem to have done a good job—I'm going back for another lot, then I'll stay here and do what I can; Jan can go back and carry on with the other men—there will be plenty of help. The plane came down in a field just beyond the village, but the ground is solid ice. The police and ambulances will take twice as long—we must do what we can...' He nodded brusquely and turned away and Henrietta went inside with her small burden.

It took a little while to get the children sorted out; there were several miraculously uninjured, and these were passed immediately to the group of women sitting ready by the great open fireplace. The others were laid gently on the blankets put ready for them and Henrietta added the toddler to the pathetic row and then bent to take a look at each of them. All but two of them had head injuries, some severe, although two appeared only lightly concussed. She set someone to watch them and turned her attention to the others; all so ill, with feeble little pulses, drawing shallow little breaths, but none of them, by some stroke of fate, burned. She covered them warmly and seeing Loes standing against the wall, called her to come and mind them. 'There's nothing you can do,' she explained, 'but you can tell me if they change in any way.'

But Loes shook her head. 'I won't,' she said. 'I do not like to see these awful things.' Her eyes filled with tears. 'I am sensitive.'

It was a waste of time to tell her that every woman in the room at that moment was feeling sensitive; Klara was hovering, so Henrietta beckoned her to take her place and got to the door as the second car arrived.

The Jonkheer met her on the top step. 'These are all badly burned—did you warn everyone?'

'Yes—how many?'

'Five—six. There are two more cars on their way. The plane was full, but there are many killed.' He started to walk away and then paused to say over his shoulder: 'Mother? She is all right?'

'She's wonderful—do you want her kept away?'

His grim face broke into a sudden smile. 'Dear girl! No—she would never forgive me, but warn them again.'

She went back into the hall and passed on his message and was glad that she had done so, for the victims carried in so carefully were a shocking sight indeed. It was to the credit of the helpers there that none of them turned away, only waited mutely to be told what to do.

This time Marnix van Hessel stayed, sending Jan back with a man from the village as he carried in the last of his passengers; a young woman, moaning a little, her face unmarked but her clothes burnt off from the waist down.

'Fractures of both legs,' he told Henrietta. 'We'll have her on the table and get them splinted.' He was already taking off his jacket and rolling up his shirt sleeves. 'Splints?'

She fetched what there was as well as scissors, and began to cut away the charred remains of the girl's skirt. 'Yes, get on with that,' he agreed, 'I'll need my bag.' He said something to a man standing nearby and bent over the girl. When the man came back, he said without looking up: 'Give those

scissors to Mevrouw Kroon—she's behind you—
and get things ready so that I can give an injec-
tion.'

It was like being back in Cas; only this was a
nightmare setting and the patients were nightmare
people. Henrietta did as he had asked and then
picked up another pair of scissors and began on
the next patient until he called her over to apply
traction on the poor burned legs while he splinted
them.

He was finishing before he spoke and then she
could see that he was voicing his thoughts, not
speaking to her. 'Plasma's what we need. I hope
they'll bring plenty with them—they won't get
here yet.' He looked at her, frowning. 'It's a mercy
that most of them are unconscious,' he muttered,
and then: 'What about the children?'

'Over here—some of them aren't too bad, I
think, they're by the fire, some of the village ladies
have them on their laps—it seemed the best thing.
The ill ones are here.'

He spent some time with them, doing what was
possible, and then, leaving Klara and her helpers
on guard, began a methodical round of the hall,
with Henrietta carrying out his instructions as best
she might, and his mother passing on his simpler
orders. Even for the badly burned, there were small
tasks to perform, little cuts to be cleaned and covered, clothes to be cut off where possible—there

were a dozen women working by now, but Loes wasn't amongst them. Henrietta was bandaging a badly cut head when the next lot of casualties were brought in—three women this time, conscious and in pain, and she hurried to draw up the injections Marnix asked for. The victims were coming in all the time now in ones and twos as more and more cars were pressed into service, and presently there were no more living, only a growing row of covered forms at the back of the hall. She was thankful that everyone was so busy that only a few had noticed the *dominee* and the priest go together behind the screen someone had thoughtfully brought.

She paused a moment and looked round her; she could recognize almost everyone she knew in the village, all helping, but she still couldn't see Loes; perhaps she was with the babies. She put down the boots she had been cutting off an elderly man and went to look, but there was no sign of her and she dismissed her from her mind and went to look at the babies by the fire; they were reacting in a reassuringly normal manner, crying and grizzling and calling for their mothers. Henrietta found it heartrending, but at least they were responding to the warmth and kindly laps and cuddling. She smiled encouragement at the small circle of women and went across the hall once more because she could hear Marnix's voice, not loud but very clear, asking for Miss Brodie.

'We'll have to do something about this,' he told her without preamble, and pulled back the blanket covering a young man with head injuries. 'Look.'

The man must have been thrown out before the plane caught fire, for he had no burns at all, only a severe concussion, and driven deep into the sleeve of his coat, a sliver of metal.

'Can't leave it; give him a shot of ATS, Henrietta, and cut as much as you can away while I get a few things.'

She was ready when he got back, his mother following him with some strips of sheet and a bowl of Savlon. He went away to wash his hands and his mother held the bowl steady while Henrietta did her best to clean up the arm. 'This won't be nice to watch,' she told the older woman gently.

'If my son can do these things and you can help him, then I am able to watch, my dear, but thank you for thinking of it. There may be some need of me here.'

There was; the metal was part of a bolt, driven in with all the force of a steam hammer, so that even Marnix's powerful hands and the bone forceps he was using made little impression. 'I'll have to cut down,' he said. 'Go and scrub, Henrietta.'

That was the second time he had called her by name; it made a nice change from his everlasting Miss Brodie. She hurried back and found that he had unwrapped some of the instruments from his bag. 'I'll cut down and tie as I go,' he told her. 'Give Mother those bits and pieces, you'll have to cut as I tie and then hold the retractors as I pull.'

She nodded and he went in his turn to scrub his hands and presently set about the tricky business, it took a few minutes and Henrietta had to admire the way he worked—fast, of course; there was no time to waste with so much to do, but all the same, with care. She clenched her teeth and held the retractors steady so that he could draw out the bolt with as little damage as possible. 'Not too much damage,' he said, 'we can explore it later—I want something to mop up with.'

Henrietta took the bits of sheet soaked in the Savlon solution from Jonkvrouw van Hessel and passed them to him. His mother, she saw, was very pale, but when she looked at her again, the little lady smiled and nodded, so that when Marnix snapped 'Penicillin' and held out an impatient hand, she felt free to take her eyes off his mother and attend to his wants; the lady might look green about the gills, but she wasn't going to faint. Her son finished his stitching. 'Firm pad and bandage—I'll leave it to you. There are the ambulances at last.'

The hall was suddenly filled with white-coated doctors and uniformed nurses, ambulance men and police; under Jonkheer van Hessel's directions they put up drips, discarded the makeshift splints and replaced them with the genuine sort, they started to carry the patients out to the ambulances. Henrietta could see Marnix, head and shoulders above everyone else, moving briskly about the hall, organizing, advising and stopping to talk to the police when they could pin him down. Everything was going ahead nicely now, there was nothing more for her to do. She took Jonkvrouw van Hessel by the arm, removed the bowl she was still clutching and walked her out of the hall into the sitting room.

'You've been marvellous,' she said warmly. 'Now you're going to sit down while I get you a drink.'

'So kind,' murmured her companion. 'That bolt…' she shuddered strongly, 'how can Marnix bear to do such awful things?'

'Well, he likes helping people so much that it gives him the strength to do such things. You must be very proud of him.' She sat his parent down in a chair and added gently: 'Now you rest, you didn't do so badly yourself, you know. I shan't be a minute.'

Henrietta had no idea where the kitchen was. She stopped a hurrying girl and asked *'Keuken?'* and was rewarded by a wave of the hand towards the back of the hall. The babies had gone, the women who had looked after them were already tidying away their chairs and folding blankets and collecting cups, but the row of blanketed figures was still there, so were the *dominee* and the priest. They looked up and smiled at her and she managed to smile back. The waved arm had indicated a door on the left; it stood open and she went through it into a wide corridor. Marnix was there and so was Loes. She was crying, gentle crying which wouldn't spoil a pretty face too much, and he had his arms around her. Henrietta slid past them and found the kitchen, a marvellous room which, had she had the time and the inclination, she would have loved to have examined at her leisure. Now she found tea and milk and sugar and a kettle on the boil, and presently took the tray she had laid back down the corridor. There was no one in it; she sighed with relief.

The hall was rapidly emptying itself and several girls, with Klara acting as forewoman, were cleaning up. Henrietta stayed with Jonkvrouw van Hessel only long enough to make sure that she was all right before going back into the hall, but this time the *dominee* stopped her and the priest joined them. They talked for a few minutes before she made her excuses, and when she turned to go it was to find Marnix standing behind her.

'I took Loes home,' he told her abruptly. 'The poor child is quite unfit for such sights and sounds—she tells me that she did her best to help, but she is sensitive and young; even the babies were too much for her tender feelings.'

Henrietta stared at him; he surely couldn't believe the rubbish he was uttering. Loes must have convinced him very thoroughly that she had done her share; well, she wasn't going to bother about that, let him think what he liked. She said shortly: 'Yes, she's very young, and it was quite dreadful.'

Suddenly she couldn't bear to be there any longer. Without another word she ran across the hall, snatched up her coat and tore through the still open door. She had quite forgotten how icy it was underfoot, and anyway, she didn't care. She ran all the way, opened her door with a shaking hand and rushed inside, to the warmth and gentle lamplight and Henry purring to see her back. Henrietta dragged off her coat and flung it down. There was the stove to see to; it had got very low, and when she looked at the clock she saw with amazement that she had been gone for more than three hours— a terrible three hours too. She sat down on the rug before the neglected stove and burst into tears. She wasn't a girl to cry often and then it was seldom for herself, but now her pent-up feelings found relief. She sobbed and sighed and gulped like a child, wiping her streaming eyes with her hands because she couldn't be bothered to find a handkerchief. She was making so much noise that she didn't hear the front door close and Jonkheer van Hessel's large, elegantly shod feet tread through the little house and come to a halt by her. She choked on an extra loud sob as he picked her up. 'My dear Miss Brodie,' he said in a calm, kind voice, 'you are the last person I expected to see giving way to tears.'

Fright at his unexpected appearance and the harrowing afternoon she had spent, combined with the vivid memory of Loes crying prettily in his arms, sent her voice spiralling upwards in rage. 'Why shouldn't I cry?' she flung at him, quite beside herself. 'Just because I'm not small and fair and blue-eyed it doesn't mean that I haven't any feelings.' She gave a great watery snort. 'Go away, do—you've no right to come into my house!'

'The key was in the lock—and you left rather suddenly, Miss Brodie.'

She sniffed. 'Well, I didn't have to wait for your permission, did I?' Her voice rose to a wail. 'Oh, do go away!'

He took no notice of this pettish demand, but pushed her gently into a chair, made up the stove and went to put the kettle on. 'Where's Henry's supper?' he asked presently, and she stopped crying to say: 'In the saucepan with the red lid.'

She sat back, her eyes closed, finding the small domestic sounds from the kitchen very soothing, and when he put a handkerchief into her hand she dried her tears and blew her pretty pinkened nose and sat up again, conscious of shame at losing her temper.

'Oh, I'm sorry,' she told him. 'You must be so tired after all that work, and driving in that fiendish weather—and your home all upset,' she gulped, 'and now me being a fool.' She added wildly: 'All those boots on that lovely floor.' She started to cry again and between the sobs said what she had really wanted to say to someone—anyone: 'Those poor people—all those babies. Why should it happen to them? And that girl with the legs...' She gave him a quite desperate look. 'And to die like that, can you imagine...and so many. Oh, Marnix!'

He whisked her out of her chair and held her closer, patting her shoulder as though she were a little girl in need of comfort. 'I know, I feel the same, but you must remember too that you have helped to save a number of lives today, and modern surgery is able to cope with the most appalling damage to a body. Even a badly burned man can become almost normal again with the help of plastic surgery.' He smiled down at her. 'And now we are going to have a cup of tea together and talk over the cases we dealt with and make a few guesses as to their chances.'

He sat her down again and fetched the tray, poured the tea and then seated himself opposite her. She was taking the first sip when she put her cup down again. 'You shouldn't be here!' she exclaimed. 'I forgot, what about your mother? She was so brave...she couldn't have seen anything so terrible in her life before. Oughtn't you to be with her?'

'Mother lived here during the German occupation; she saw a good deal which was—unpleasant, shall we say? I gave her something to calm her and send her to sleep for an hour or two. Klara is with her.'

'Oh, I see. I'm sorry if she's very upset, because she was wonderful, but so was everyone—and they were all so quick, and no one looked away when the casualties were brought in—they deserve medals for that.' She took another heartening sip, finding it helped enormously to talk about it. 'Where have they gone?'

'Tilburg and Eindhoven and a few to Breda— they will let me know in an hour or two how things are and I shall be going to see for myself later on. I doubt if any of them will be fit for theatre until tomorrow.'

'How many of them have a chance?'

He set down his tea cup and sat back, relaxed and matter-of-fact. 'Now let us see—the children first; they all have a good chance. Fractured skulls are nasty but not necessarily fatal, although I imagine that several of them will need surgery. I am always lost in wonder at the resilience of the small child to injury and disease. As to the other cases, let me see...' He was easing the talk along without her realizing it, not dwelling unnecessarily on the worst bits, but pointing out the most likely cases to recover.

Presently he got to his feet. 'I have to go—there are other visits,' and she nodded. Loes, of course; he must have been dying to get away. She said brightly: 'Oh, yes, thank you for staying, it was kind of you.'

He was putting on his sheepskin jacket, not looking at her. 'If you feel you would rather not be alone here, my mother wished me to tell you that you will be very welcome at the castle—there is plenty of room.'

'She's very kind, but I'm quite all right, thank you.' Henrietta was anxious for him to be gone now; the thought that he would hurry straight to Loes, and the fact that he hadn't added his own invitation to that of his mother, hurt very much; he must still dislike her, and his kindness was something he would have offered to anyone in need of it in like circumstance. She preceded him to the door and wished him good night and smiled from a tear-stained face.

'Thank you for all you did today.' He had paused in the tiny hall. 'You organized everything with great efficiency, not an easy thing to do at a moment's notice. I am greatly indebted to you, Miss Brodie.'

How formal he was with his Miss Brodie—well, she could be formal too. 'I'm glad that I was of some help, Jonkheer van Hessel.'

He grinned suddenly. 'I haven't been called Jonkheer so often in years,' he observed, half laughing.

She opened the door. 'No? And nor have I been called Miss Brodie so incessantly—but it acts nicely as a reminder not to get too friendly, doesn't it? Not that there's much danger of that.'

He paused once more. 'A debatable point. Perhaps it might take our minds off other things if we were to discuss it.'

'Now now, Loes will be waiting for you.' She made her voice sound casual.

'Will she?' His eyes had narrowed, he was looking just about as bad-tempered as he ever had done.

She said a little wearily: 'Of course. It's only natural.'

'Why?'

She looked at him with a mixture of exasperation and impatience. 'Well, she depends on you, you must know that—I mean, when you're going to marry someone...'

'Am I?' His voice was remote.

'Loes told me...' She stopped; possibly she wasn't supposed to know, although the girl hadn't sworn her to secrecy. 'I'm sorry, it's none of my business.'

'You are quite right, Miss Brodie, it is not.' The grey eyes were cold, as was his voice. Their truce, brought about by the dreadful happenings of the afternoon, was over.

After he had gone Henrietta went back to the stove and sat down on the floor with Henry curled up against her. She stayed there for a long time, not wishing for any supper and only getting up at length to go to bed.

She didn't see Marnix van Hessel for three days, although each morning Jan appeared at the door, sent with news of the victims—sparse news delivered in his still more sparse English, but she was grateful for it, especially as they had parted on bad terms. There had been reporters at the door too, but these she had treated with brief politeness, refusing to be drawn into talk of the disaster; there were surely people enough to tell them all they wanted to know. There had been a lot of talk in the village, naturally enough, and when she had gone to the shop she had found herself the centre of a circle of smiling women, expressing admiration for her part in the rescue work, and she had thanked them in her faulty Dutch, feeling shy, and then listened to the countless versions of the crash. A great deal she was unable to understand, but one fact emerged over and over again; Jonkheer van

Hessel had visited each and every one of them and thanked them personally for their help, and if her Dutch wasn't at fault, he had paid for the blankets and sheets which had been offered so generously, and as for the men who had left their work in order to help, he had himself made up the wages they had lost. The women nodded and smiled as they talked, making her one of themselves; she had been accepted as a member of the village, she realized with a glow of pleasure. They had always been kind to her, perhaps because Marnix had introduced her to them in the first place, but now she had been accepted on her own merits. She went home feeling happier than she had done for days.

It was the following day that Jonkvrouw van Hessel paid her a visit. Henrietta had finished her chores, built a good fire in the stove and had gone to make the coffee, and when someone knocked on the door she wasn't surprised; it was about the time that Jan came with his news. She went to the door expecting him and the surprise on her face caused her visitor to exclaim: 'Good morning, Henrietta, I have surprised you—you see I have accepted your invitation to call on you although I come without warning. I hope that you do not mind too much, but I wished to talk.'

She had followed Henrietta into the dining-room and paused to look around her. 'Nothing is changed, and that is nice...but that is not what I was saying. I wished to talk so badly, but Marnix—well, he is tired. He spends the whole day at one or other of the hospitals and when he comes home he shuts himself in his study. That, in the circumstances, is natural enough, but it gives me no chance to talk, and so I inflict myself upon you, my dear. You do not mind, I hope?'

'No, I'm very glad, and I hadn't anything planned, really I hadn't. I am becoming idle.'

'You were not idle the other day, my dear. I am full of admiration for your calm and good sense and kindness, and so are those who live in the village. You have filled your aunt's shoes to perfection, Henrietta.'

Henrietta went a little pink. 'Oh, how nice of you to say so. Won't you sit down? Jan has been each morning with news, but not very much, and of course I can't read the papers. The reporters have been here too, but I didn't care to talk to them.'

Her visitor had seated herself by the stove and Henrietta went to hang up her coat. 'No, I know—tiresome men, though they have their work to do, no doubt. And the television too, all so public—the village did not like that.'

She accepted the coffee Henrietta offered her. 'This is most delightful,' she declared. 'You are sure that you are not wishing me to go?'

'Indeed, no, *mevrouw*, it will be nice to have a

talk. I think we would forget it more easily if we discussed it all.'

'Yes—I see it all so vividly still.' She opened the crocodile handbag Henrietta had been secretly admiring and drew out a newspaper cutting. 'I have brought something to read to you, for it concerns you, my dear. Marnix was interviewed, most unwillingly—but he made it very plain that he could not have managed without your help, and that he and the village are most grateful to you. He also expressed the hope that you would remain with us.'

Henrietta had gone a little pale. 'That was very kind of him, but quite unnecessary.'

'You do not perhaps wish to stay with us for always?'

'Oh, I do—I couldn't bear—that is, I should like to very much, but I'm not sure—you see, I'll have to start earning my living again.' She added anxiously, 'I haven't told anyone else that.'

'You mean that you haven't told Marnix,' her guest corrected her calmly. 'Don't worry, I shall not tell him either.' She was folding the cutting neatly and didn't look up. 'He is very engrossed in his work, and when he is not at the hospital or his rooms or managing his affairs here, he is with Loes Rietveld. Perhaps he thinks that he is in love with her. I doubt that, but I do not know. But I do know that if he were to marry her, my heart would break. She is a selfish, shallow girl with no heart, you see, and he is none of these things. He has many faults, but none that the right girl cannot cure for him.' The pretty voice held contempt. 'I saw the other afternoon how badly she behaved. She is no fit wife for my son.'

'She's very young.'

'And what has that to do with it?' For a moment the Jonkvrouw sounded like her son. 'What has age to do with it? Am I, because I am an elderly woman of sixty-five or so, expected to view without emotion bodies with arms and legs so burned that they cannot be recognized as such, or take no notice of children with their heads crushed? You too, Henrietta, you are a nurse and possibly you have seen such horrors before, but do not tell me that they did not horrify you so that you wanted to turn and run?'

'You're quite right—I'd have given anything not to have been there, but all the same...'

'There is no excuse for the girl, she is not the stuff to make van Hessels.' The Jonkvrouw made a sound, half sob, half snort. 'And Marnix believes her to be sweet and kind and soft-hearted. Bah!'

Henrietta eyed her visitor with interest. She had always liked the little lady and since she had witnessed her calm behaviour with the victims of the plane crash, she had respect for her too. Now she found herself wanting to put her arms round her and comfort her. She said at length: 'I'm sorry you are unhappy about your son, but he's not young any more. He must surely know his own mind and I imagine he's not easily persuaded.'

His parent shot her an eloquent glance. 'How right you are,' she said crisply, 'and it's just because he is no longer young that he feels he should marry. Understand, Henrietta, that I wish very much that he would take a wife, but not that chit of a selfish girl.' Jonkvrouw van Hessel shook her pretty head with great determination and paused to reflect. 'A long time ago now, he was in love with a girl, a handsome wilful creature—of course they quarrelled and at first it didn't matter very much, and then they had no love left, no liking even for each other. And since that time he has never thought of marriage—oh, he has had girl-friends, but none who mattered, and now there is Loes, small and helpless and malleable—that is the word?—only she is none of these things, although she pretends to them, so that he is delighted that he has found a girl who will agree with him always, do exactly as he wishes—not choosing to admit, even to himself that if she did, he would dislike it very much and very soon he would discover what she is really like.' She sighed deeply. 'I do not know why I bother you with my troubles, perhaps because your aunt and I were good friends and you do not seem like a stranger to me.' She put down her cup and got to her feet. 'You have been kind, listening to an old woman's grumbles. One day soon I hope that you will come and see me again.'

They walked to the door together and there she paused to say: 'I am glad that I came, for I feel much better about everything—perhaps there will be a happy ending, after all.' She smiled and shook hands and walked off briskly, turning back at the castle gates to wave, and Henrietta, watching her from her door, waved back. She must not, she told herself, allow a decided fondness for Marnix's mother to override her other feelings; life was difficult enough as it was. She longed to be someone with a cool nature, not easily touched by emotion. Perhaps with a little determination she could change herself into just such a type; it shouldn't be too difficult for she saw little enough of Marnix and when they did meet, they always disagreed, or almost always. He gave her no encouragement to foster any warmth towards him, so it should be easy.

CHAPTER SIX

IT wasn't easy at all; after a couple of days during which she did her best to be detached and cool and pretend that she didn't love Marnix at all, she reverted to her true self once more, which allowed her to think of him all the time if she wanted to, and imagine a number of happenings which would culminate in a happy ending, instead of the real life finale, when she would have to find a home for Henry, pack her bags and go back to England and work again. It might be a good thing, she reasoned during her more sensible surveys of her future, if she were to let the house and later—years later, when she had grown used to the idea of Marnix and Loes being married—she might come back, but in her more irresponsible moments she saw herself remaining at Gijzelmortel, working at some hospital nearby, miraculously sprung up overnight to accommodate her, with Henry for company, and Charlie—most certainly not garaged at the castle, carefully preserved so that she could go to Tilburg whenever she wished. The job would have to be something not too demanding at hours to suit herself and she would live very comfortably, avoiding Marnix at all costs. Which brought her back to thinking about him again.

The weather didn't help either; it was still cold, with a sneering wind and icy rain, not the weather for long walks. Henrietta was forced to content herself with visits to the shop for exercise and a great deal of piano playing. But within a few days the weather brightened so that she decided to spend the morning out of doors. There were several small villages she had heard of and never seen; she would take the opportunity of seeking them out before the rain started again. She put on slacks and a thick sweater and the boots, ate her breakfast quickly, and was on the point of washing the dishes when someone thundered on the door knocker. Jan with news or the postman—it was far too early for a social visit. She went to the door, a tea towel in her hand, and opened it.

Marnix van Hessel stalked in, took the door from her grasp, shut it and swept her back into the dining-room.

'Good morning,' said Henrietta pointedly, and when he didn't speak: 'Have you lost your tongue, Jonkheer van Hessel? Do you know that it vexes me very much that you can never bring yourself to wish me good day or good-bye? Such a lack of good manners in a man of your position is to be deplored.'

He turned to stare at her. 'Good God, you sound

like a schoolmarm! I've come to take you to see some of the patients who were here.'

She bristled. 'Is that an invitation or an order?' she wanted to know.

He smiled suddenly and his whole face changed so that her treacherous heart bounced against her ribs. 'My dear good...' He saw the expression on her face and laughed outright. 'Henrietta, I thought that you might like to see how the people you helped are progressing. I've calls to make at all three hospitals, you could have a quick peep at some of them, maybe it will help you to forget the awful things you had to see and do. I should have asked you before this, perhaps, but I've been busy...if you have other plans, I'll invite you another day.'

She heard herself saying weakly: 'Thank you, I'd like to come very much, but you'll have to wait a few minutes—I must see to Henry and I can't go like this.'

He eyed her without haste and she coloured faintly. 'Why not? You'll need a coat and something on your head, it's cold still. I'll see to Henry while you get your things.'

Perhaps her clothes wouldn't matter after all; they would only be going to the hospitals and no one would notice her. She made for the stairs, calling over her shoulder: 'There's porridge in the saucepan for Henry, and he'll need some fresh milk, and if we are to be gone for more than an hour or two he had better have some of that fishy stuff in the tin.'

By the time she got downstairs again he had seen to it all and made up the stove besides, and he waited patiently while she said good-bye to the kitten, made sure that the back door was locked, looked in her handbag to make sure that she had the key and took a last look at herself in the mirror. 'I'm ready,' she declared, and allowed herself to be ushered out of the house into the Rolls, all her fine resolutions forgotten.

He took her first to Tilburg, and the conversation, naturally enough, was of the air crash and its consequences, but presently he asked her: 'Have you see Loes since then?'

'No,' said Henrietta carefully, not wanting to spoil their harmonious mood, 'but I haven't been out, only to the shop, and I shouldn't think she would want to go out either, it's been such beastly weather…'

She was given no chance to pursue this harmless topic. 'She is unhappy,' her companion informed her. 'She feels that she has let everyone down, that she didn't do sufficient to help, although from what she told me she did more than her share. Nothing I can say has altered her feelings about it. It would be kind of you, Miss Brodie, if you would go and see her and make her understand that she did a splendid job. She admires you greatly, you know, indeed she told me that she hopes that when she is your age, she will have acquired your strength of character.'

The cat—the nasty little cat! fumed Henrietta, and such a clever one too. Now he thinks of me like that, I suppose, a bit long in the tooth, the born maiden aunt. Aloud she said, her voice level: 'How sweet of her, but so inaccurate. It isn't strength of character, you know, only bad temper.'

She saw his sharp, puzzled glance, but he didn't answer her, only remarked that they were almost at the hospital.

Henrietta had supposed in a vague fashion that he would consign her to the care of one of the Ward Sisters, or at most, take her himself to visit one or two chosen patients. She hadn't expected the little group of people hovering in the entrance hall as they entered. They were introduced to her with meticulous good manners by Marnix—registrar, housemen, a handful of students. She shook hands with each of them in turn and cast him a smouldering glance as she took off her headscarf and tried to do something to her wildly curling hair; she must look a perfect fright, she thought indignantly, and had the thought answered by his quiet: 'No need to look at me like that, Henrietta. You look beautiful—but of course you know that already.'

She gaped at him in surprise as he took her arm and propelled her gently towards the handsome staircase before them, and he kept a large, firm hand under her elbow as they went up in a group, unhurriedly, while he expounded something or other in his own language and the bodyguard murmured its agreement. There were wide arched doors at either end of the corridor they reached and they turned to the left. Women's Surgical, she was told as the doors opened and another group was discovered—Sister, nurses, physio... Her eye moved from one to the other, all looking reassuringly like her colleagues at home.

Marnix had cast off his coat in the hall. Now, very elegant in his dark grey suiting, he greeted these ladies, performed more introductions and moved off down the ward, Henrietta in tow. True, he had relinquished her arm, but at the same time had bidden her stay beside him in a quiet voice so charged with authority that she obeyed without question and only in the nick of time prevented herself from addressing him as sir.

The ward was modern, with glassed-off cubicles, and they passed several of these before they stopped. The occupant of the bed was a girl Henrietta remembered very well. She had cut that fair hair around the deep gash in the girl's head, cleaned it and then stood by, helping while Marnix had stitched it, and she remembered the girl's badly burned hands too. It was nice to see her smiling now. Her face was white and weary from the shock and pain she had gone through, but she must have made a joke, because everyone laughed as she waved her burned hands in their sterile envelopes. So they used the Bunyan-Stannard method, too, did they? And in this case it appeared to be very successful. Marnix was bending over the girl now and presently he turned round to say: 'You remember her, don't you? She thanks you for your care of her. She is doing very well indeed; in a short time we shall send her to a burns unit and her hands will receive further treatment.'

Henrietta murmured and smiled and longed to speak Dutch so that she could say something, and was grateful to Marnix for his smooth handling of the few awkward words she uttered. The girl smiled and nodded and they moved on, out into the ward again.

There were three more girls in the ward and two toddlers in the children's unit downstairs. 'These two have done very well,' Marnix explained to her, and indeed they seemed a far cry from the unhappy children she had seen at the castle. 'And now come and see the men.'

There were six of them, two of them American, who greeted her with a cheerful 'Hi,' and kept her talking for some minutes. They had been severely burned and once they had been pronounced fit enough they too would be given skin grafts; meanwhile they were cheerful enough. They remembered very little about it, they assured her, although one of them was positive that he remembered her getting the boots off his feet.

They all had coffee after that, crowded into Sister's office, and although most of them spoke Dutch to each other, those nearest her took care to carry on a conversation in English, so that Henrietta felt at home. Indeed, she was quite sorry to leave, but there was still Breda to visit and after that, Eindhoven. She occupied their short journey with sensible comments on the cases she had just seen, and her companion seemed content to let her do this, supplying information when she requested it and offering an undoubted learned opinion when she asked for one. Exactly like the brief, businesslike discussions she and God used to have after they had done a round on Women's Medical, she remembered, but keeping to technicalities seemed the best thing, for on the subjects of surgery and medicine she recognized him as a master, and there was no fear of them falling out.

They reached the next hospital on the best of terms and here the procedure was repeated, only there were many more patients to visit and one or two of them were still seriously ill. They drank another cup of coffee too while Marnix held a brief discussion with an elderly man, stoutly built and balding, and as the Ward Sister told her, a professor.

'How nice,' said Henrietta inanely, lost for a more imaginative Dutch adjective and trying not to look too often at Marnix.

'Indeed, yes—a clever man, but then so is Professor van Hessel clever also.'

'Oh, is he? I didn't know—but I didn't know that he was a surgeon until quite recently, either.'

She waited while the Ward Sister, a serious student of the English language and a stickler for the right answers, thought this over.

'You are not bosom friends?' she wanted to know, and Henrietta choked back a laugh and assured her gravely that no, hardly that; it was only because she was a nurse and the Jonkheer had asked for her help and then had most kindly offered to let her see some of the patients to whom she had given first aid.

Her companion looked disappointed and Henrietta was relieved that she should be summoned at that moment to take her leave. 'We have to be in Eindhoven by half past two,' stated Marnix sternly, just as though she were the one who had prevented their prompt departure, but she followed him out meekly enough after a round of handshaking, and got into the Rolls beside him in a compliant manner which caused him to eye her with suspicion. 'Why do you look so damned submissive?' he demanded of her.

She turned an indignant look on him. 'Well, whatever next—when I've been doing my best to be the pattern of docile behaviour, and since we're picking holes in each other, let me tell you that you could have at least told me that I wasn't suitably dressed...'

'Ah, so that's it. I thought I had made it quite clear to you that it wouldn't matter if you were draped in a sack, Miss Brodie; you are fortunate enough to have the looks to make anything else unnecessary.'

She looked away, muttering crossly and staring out of the window; he made it impossible for her to answer him. Presently she said stiffly: 'I'm sorry. I'm really very grateful to you for letting me see the patients; it's made me feel quite different about the whole awful thing.'

'I knew it would. Do you suppose we might remain on speaking terms long enough to have lunch together?'

She had to laugh then and he gave her a grin which took ten years from his face. 'There's a nice old-fashioned place in Eindhoven, we'll go there.'

It wasn't in the least old-fashioned; it was a very superior restaurant indeed called Au Carré des Champignons, in the Hotel Schimmelpenninck, but when she told him that his idea of old-fashioned wasn't hers and that he had overlooked that she wasn't dressed for such a place, he remarked blandly: 'Oh, but it is old-fashioned,' and took her by the arm and led her outside on to the pavement where they stood in a biting wind while he pointed out the salient points of its undoubtedly bygone architecture.

'You really are a most annoying man,' she told him. She spoke through her teeth because they had begun to chatter with the cold, but all he did was laugh a little.

'Now, Henrietta, remember we have to remain friends until we have eaten our lunch,' and he marched her back into the restaurant again, told her to go away and pretty herself up a bit and when she looked around her in a hesitant way, gave her a gentle push. 'Over there—go on, I'll be here when you get back.'

When she returned he was standing with his back to her and she paused a moment to look at him; even from that viewpoint he was a striking figure and outstandingly elegant. She sighed because she loved him so much, and when he turned round quickly she only just had the time to assume the cool expression which would meet the occasion. It couldn't have been quite as cool as she had thought, for he came to meet her with the air of being delighted to see her again. 'You look very nice,' and he sounded so convinced of this that she actually forgot that she was in slacks and a sweater. 'Come and have a drink.'

She didn't know much about drinks; Roger Thorpe had always ordered a sweet sherry for her without asking her first, and so, now that she came to think about it, had most of the other men she had been out with. She said now: 'Thank you,' and when he asked her what she would like, said 'Sherry,' doubtfully, adding by way of explanation: 'I've always been given that.'

She smiled briefly and looked away, feeling foolish and old-maidish, so that she didn't see the expression on his face; amused in a kindly way and then suddenly tender. 'Well, shall I be the first one to suggest something else?' His voice was nicely matter-of-fact. 'A Dubonnet, perhaps? If you don't like it you must say so and we'll try something else.'

He lifted a finger at the hovering waiter and gave the order and she asked: 'Are you going to drink that too?'

He looked at her gravely. 'All Dutchmen drink gin before dinner,' he assured her.

Henrietta liked the drink when it came, she liked the white Burgundy which they drank with their lobster soufflé, which delicacy she ate with a splendid appetite, just as she did the Barossa tart which followed it, a confection of fruits and cream cheese tastefully arranged in a delicate pastry case, and not being worried by weight problems, she enjoyed the lashings of whipped cream which went with it, but most of all she enjoyed their conversations. She had had no idea that her companion could be so dryly humorous or so entertaining; she forgot how grumpy he could be; she forgot, almost, that she was in love with him and allowed herself to enjoy the present. She told him with an endearing candour that she had enjoyed her lunch as they sat over coffee and he smiled lazily at her.

'I'm glad, although I am sure that you have been lunched and dined many times, Miss Brodie.'

'Well, yes—but none of them were like you,' she informed him with a frankness engendered by the Burgundy. He didn't laugh but said gently: 'Why, thank you, Henrietta, and may I return the compliment and say that I, too, found none of my previous companions like you?' They looked at each other for a long minute, then he said briskly: 'We should be going—I am to meet a friend of mine at the hospital, he's a first-rate plastic surgeon. We have high hopes of being able to do a great deal for one of the patients who will need his services for some time to come, I'm afraid.'

So after that they talked shop once more, until he drew up outside the hospital and ushered her in through its doors. It was a large modern building and she looked around her as much as she was able as he hurried her across the large entrance hall.

'The wards first,' she was told, 'and then perhaps you might like to look around the place while I have a word with Schiller.'

So she was borne along with a group of people very similar to those in the other two hospitals, only this time, once they had taken the rather crowded journey in a startlingly rapid lift to the fifth floor, they were joined by a grey-bearded gentleman who twinkled nicely at her when they were introduced and called her dear lady, which made her feel small and fragile and exquisitely dressed. It was a pity, she mused as they went into the ward, that Marnix didn't say things like that, though probably he did to Loes. She remembered that twice that day he had told her that she was beautiful and frowned a little; he had a sarcastic turn of speech at times and probably he hadn't meant a word of it. She would have liked time to have meditated about this, but they had reached a long line of cubicles and someone had opened a door.

To a whispered warning: 'This one is bad, I'm afraid,' she went inside, Marnix's hand under her elbow, and when he gave it a squeeze, she was under no illusion that he was doing it for personal reasons, only to re-affirm his warning. The man in the bed was going to need a great deal done to him before his face would be bearable again, but his eyes had been spared, so she smiled at him and sat down close to his bed. He was an American, she had been told, which made it easier.

'You don't remember me,' she told him cheerfully. 'I'm from the village where your plane crashed and we all wanted to know how you were getting on. Jon…Professor van Hessel brought me along.'

The man couldn't answer, but he winked, which seemed like an invitation to talk for a few minutes. Henrietta chattered away, wondering with pity what he did to occupy his long days and nights; his fractured jaws were wired, his hands bandaged—and yet he had the courage to wink. She got up finally, saying she would like to come and see him again, and this time he winked with such enthusiasm that she winked back.

'He'll get better?' she asked when they were out of earshot.

'Yes—we'll have to reshape a good deal of his face and try and do something about his hands. He'll never be as good as new, I'm afraid, but he'll pass muster.' They had stopped at another door. 'This lady is doing quite nicely—burns, of course, but not too bad on the face—mostly neck and shoulders. An American too.'

She spent a little longer here, for the patient wanted to talk, and Henrietta listened with sympathy and a patience which was only brought to a close by the remembrance that Marnix wished to consult with the grey-bearded Mr Schiller, so she spent the next hour in the capable hands of a pretty young Ward Sister who took her on a thorough tour of the hospital, explaining everything in precise English and delighted to find that Henrietta was more than ready to air her basic Dutch. It was too good an opportunity to miss, for she knew a good many words by now even though her pronunciation was faulty, to say the least—here was someone her own age, only too delighted to correct her.

They were firm friends by the time they got back to the consultants' room on the ground floor, where both learned gentlemen were still deeply engrossed, although Marnix got to his feet when she went in, but only long enough to ask her to sit down. 'We shan't be long,' he added, and plunged once more into their discussion.

Henrietta sat composedly in an outsize leather chair and occupied her time in going over the additions to her vocabulary, and was rewarded for her patience by a charming little speech of thanks from the older man and a terse: 'Thanks', from Marnix.

They discussed the cases she had seen at some length during the drive back to Gijzelmortel, and after one or two attempts to change the conversation to a lighter topic, she gave up. It was apparent that her companion had no wish to change the subject; he was no longer the amusing companion who had shared her lunch—indeed, he behaved as though he couldn't get home fast enough and so be rid of her company. It was all the more surprising therefore when he drove past her own front door, swept the Rolls through the castle gates and over the bridge and stopped outside its entrance.

It seemed a strange thing to do after his almost impatient manner during their drive from Eindhoven; he could have stopped so easily at her house. She undid her seat belt and got out of the car, sniffing the first chill of frost, for the afternoon was fading fast even though the sky was clear overhead. 'Thanks for a delightful day,' she said across the car's elegant bonnet, 'though perhaps delightful isn't quite the word—but it was satisfying to see those terrible injuries dealt with and know that they've a chance...I'll say good...' She was cut short.

'My mother will never forgive me if I don't bring you in to tea, she will wish to hear about everything.'

'Some other time,' Henrietta heard her voice, most satisfyingly normal, and turned to go, to find her way barred, for he had come round the Rolls very fast to stop her. 'Don't be hoity-toity,' he advised crisply. 'I can see that you are by the way your chin is stuck in the air. Why?'

'I do not like to be ordered to do this, that and

the other, especially when you were so anxious to get here. You couldn't have demonstrated your eagerness to get rid of me more plainly, and now you expect me to come into your house just because you say so.' Her voice rose a little. 'There is no will you or would you about your invitations, Jonkheer van Hessel, they're more in the nature of a command, and I don't care for that. I'm grateful to you for taking me today and for giving me such a splendid lunch—I've thanked you for that, now I shall go home. I'll visit your mother later in the week.'

He hadn't budged an inch during this lengthy speech; now he said on hidden laughter: 'I should look a fool on my knees before you, Miss Brodie, but if that is how you like your invitations, then I will get down on them here and now.' And he actually made a movement so that she put out a protesting hand, crying on the edge of laughter: 'Don't be absurd, you'll do no such thing, and since you are so insistent, I'll come in and see your mother.'

She couldn't see his face plainly in the dusk, but she fancied that he was smiling as he caught her by the arm and opened the great door.

His mother wasn't alone. Loes was with her. They both looked up as Henrietta went in to the sitting-room and their instant relief at having their tête-à-tête interrupted was patent to her eye, although there was no trace of expression on the older lady's face, but Loes looked sulky, an expression which she changed to a hurt smile and an aggrieved look of resigned patience as she jumped up and went to meet Marnix. Of Henrietta she took no notice at all.

'Marnix—I said that I would come this afternoon to return your book, did you forget?' She spoke in English—an attempt, thought Henrietta nastily, to make her appear inferior to the rest of them. She crossed the room to greet her hostess, suddenly quite sure that Marnix hadn't forgotten at all; he had known that Loes would be here. She wondered how he was going to get out of it, and heard him say coolly: 'I took Henrietta to visit some of my patients. They're doing rather well, you know.'

Listening to Jonkvrouw van Hessel's gentle chatter, Henrietta watched Loes, admiring the attractive way she wrinkled her nose while she said in a little girl voice: 'I'm still trying to forget those terrible things I saw and did.' And she looked such a picture of innocent pity that she longed to shake the girl. She turned her shoulder instead and said: 'Your son insisted that I should come in, although I daresay it is very inconvenient to you, *mevrouw*.'

'No, my dear—certainly not, I am most pleased to see you. Pull the bell rope, would you? We will have tea—a little late, but I am sure that Marnix never thought to give you any.'

Henrietta sat down on the sofa beside the older lady. 'Well, no, he didn't, but he was busy consulting with someone—a Professor Schiller, a nice man with a beard—and then he seemed anxious to come home. I daresay he wanted to see Loes.' She looked directly at her companion, who looked back at her without speaking, nonetheless conveying the pleasing knowledge that she was a firm ally. She jumped only slightly when Marnix spoke from directly behind her.

'Mother, you have waited tea for us—how kind, but Loes tells me that she must return home now. Nothing I can say will persuade her to do otherwise—I'm sure that if you had known that she couldn't stay, you would have ordered tea earlier.'

His manners were very good, thought Henrietta, his courteous voice almost concealed his annoyance, and she had to admire his mother's sweet: 'Why, Marnix, of course I would have done so, but I had no idea that Loes wished to return home so urgently. I have rung for tea just this minute. Surely she can stay a little longer?'

She smiled at Loes, who turned her head away, and it was Marnix who answered. 'She insists on going now—I'll run her back in the car.' He cast a baleful eye on Henrietta, just as though the whole thing were her doing. 'I shall be back within a few minutes, Miss Brodie.'

Henrietta opened her lovely eyes wide and looked at him with a charming smile. 'I can hardly wait,' she told him, and listened with satisfaction to his quickdrawn breath.

Loes bade them good-bye, still sulkily, and the tea was brought in. The two ladies settled down to enjoy it—an English tea; tiny sandwiches, little cakes, fingers of toast. They were about to drink their second cups when the master of the castle returned, looking like a thundercloud. He accepted tea, ate several pieces of toast and contributed no more to the conversation than was absolutely necessary, while his two companions, who loved him, each in her own way, more than anything else in the world, carried on their inconsequential chatter. It was when the tea things had been taken away that Jonkvrouw van Hessel demanded: 'And now, Henrietta, I should like to hear about the people you visited today, the memory of them has worried me a good deal, and I hope that you will be able to reassure me. Marnix has done so a dozen times, but he sees them as a surgeon, whereas you see them as men and women.'

Henrietta glanced at Marnix, who was sitting back in his chair, half asleep. 'We went to Tilburg first,' she began, and then related the day's happenings faithfully, stressing the more optimistic side of things and playing down the less hopeful. 'So you see,' she ended, 'they have all got a chance; they looked ghastly when they were here, but now, in hospital, clean and cared for and properly treated for their injuries, they're people again, if you see what I mean, so none of it was wasted. The things you had to see and do—they were all worth while, so now you can forget that part of it and think about them getting better.'

'You must have been a good Ward Sister, my dear—such calm common sense and kindness and a pretty face—and a way of making people believe you too—not that I haven't believed every word you have uttered. If I were ill, I should like you to look after me.'

'Oh, would you? What a nice thing to say— thank you. And now I think I should be going, Henry will want his supper.'

She got to her feet and shook hands, but not with Marnix, who hadn't uttered a word; Henrietta gave him a chilly smile and a still chillier good-bye, so that it was all the more disconcerting that he should go to the door with her and accompany her across the hall. At the entrance door she paused momentarily and said again: 'Well, good-bye, Jonkheer van Hessel,' which proved to be a waste of breath, for he had snatched up his coat from a chair and was going through the door with her.

'There is no need to come out,' she assured him

briskly. 'The drive is well lighted, and my house is only a stone's throw away.'

It was like talking to the wind, for he made no answer, merely swept her along beside him, down to the gates and round the corner to her own front door, where he put out a hand for the key, opened it for her and stood aside for her to go in before stalking in himself. Before she had time to speak he asked irritably: 'Why do you vex me, Miss Brodie? Why do you stoke up the sparks of my ill temper—and why do you not like Loes?'

She left the first part of his question prudently unanswered, allowing her eyes to widen into an innocent stare. 'Me?' she repeated, 'not like Loes? And since we're asking questions, why did you pretend that you didn't know that she would be there this afternoon, when she was?'

He frowned. 'What makes you say that? Why should you think it?'

'Oh, I can read people's faces,' she told him lightly.

'Indeed? Then take a good look at mine, Miss Brodie.'

It was unnerving to study his face, his cool eyes, his impressive nose, his firm mouth and the stubborn chin beneath it, but she did so because he had more or less challenged her... She was quite unprepared for his sudden swoop and the fierce kiss, so that she had nothing to say when he asked softly: 'Well, Henrietta, did you read that in my face? Because if you did you're looking mighty taken aback about it now.'

He had gone, shutting the door gently behind him.

CHAPTER SEVEN

MIJNHEER VAN DER ZANDE called the next morning just as Henrietta was making herself some coffee, so naturally enough he sat down and had a cup with her. He had come, he explained carefully, to see how she was; he had been away when the plane had crashed, but he had heard on all sides that she had excelled herself in doing her duty. She could think of no answer to this somewhat pompous observation, so she inquired where he had been. 'Holidays?' she wanted to know.

His answer was as earnest as his face. 'Certainly not. Jonkheer van Hessel has property in Friesland—a small farm. When he is too busy to go himself, I go in his stead, to make sure that it goes well.'

She refilled his cup. 'It seems to me that you have a great deal to do.'

He looked shocked. 'That is not so, Miss Brodie,' and he looked so put out that she hastened to change the conversation. 'How is your young lady—Engelina?'

He brightened. 'She is well. I saw her on my way back here, just for a short time.'

'Oh, good. When are you meeting her again?'

He looked so downcast that she was instantly sorry for him. 'Difficulties?' she wanted to know.

'It is hard to meet—my mother...I should like her to stay with us, but my mother will not hear of it. If Jonkheer van Hessel were to meet her I know that he would like her immediately and perhaps he would persuade my mother; there may be some house or other in the village within the next year or so; she wouldn't have to go far away and we could see her every day. Engelina and I would be very happy in the house I have now.' He sighed.

He was rather a poppet, sitting there waving his coffee cup at her, wanting so badly to break away from his formidable parent and not sure how to set about it. She smiled suddenly. 'I say, I've just had a super idea; your Engelina can come and stay here and then you can come and see her just as often as you want to, and when the right moment comes, you can introduce her to the boss and set the ball rolling.'

'Set the ball? I do not understand.'

She explained. 'And don't leave it too long, for I shall have to go back to England sooner or later, you know, and it would be nice to have it all settled first. Telephone Engelina and see what she says—no one needs to know that she's here, and you can pop in and out...what about her parents? Do they approve of you?'

He answered eagerly: 'Oh, yes—I have not

asked them formally, but I think they would like Engelina to marry me.'

'Then that's settled. Let me know when she would like to come and I'll get the room ready.'

He got to his feet. 'You are most kind, Miss Brodie—you do not mind that you should do this?'

'I will just love the company,' she told him as she ushered him out of the house, and then went to sit at her desk and work out just how much more money it would take to feed two instead of one. It wouldn't be for long—a week or two, perhaps, and it might help matters. The sums came out quite nicely; she put on her outdoor things and went off to the shop to buy her groceries and air her Dutch.

It was two days before she saw Marnix van Hessel again. She had gone for a walk after her lunch and was picking her way over the cobbled square when he came out of the castle gates, striding towards her.

'I wanted to see you,' he began without preamble, and came to a halt in front of her so that unless she dodged round him, she had to stop too. She wished him good afternoon in a pointed manner and waited. The brisk exercise had given her cheeks a becoming glow and her eyes sparkled, though more with temper than good health; it was wonderful to meet him suddenly like this, but why did he have to irritate her with his terse greeting—it wasn't a greeting at all, merely a statement; she wondered uneasily if he had got to hear about her plans for having Engelina to stay and was going to voice his disapproval. She braced herself for an argument, but it wasn't that at all.

'When do you intend returning to England?' he asked.

Henrietta goggled at him. 'Me? Go back to England?' she reiterated foolishly. 'I don't know. Why do you ask?'

He brushed this aside. 'You have sufficient money for how long?—four months? Six? There is a part-time job at the Rusthuis in the next village—Hoogshot—it's a very small place, tucked away in the woods, but it's central for all the old people who have lived hereabouts all their lives, they like to end their days where they belong and close to their families. It isn't a Sister's post, only a helper; someone to get them up and dressed and moving in the morning. The girl who has been doing that is leaving to get married, and I wondered if you would care to take on the job. The pay isn't very much, but it might suffice to eke out what you have for a little longer.'

She was surprised at that; she would have thought that he would have been pleased to see her go; on the other hand, if they hadn't got anyone else in view, it might suit his convenience—anyway, it would be an experience and the extra money would certainly mean that she could stay a good deal longer. She stamped her feet, for it was cold standing there in the biting wind. 'May I think it over?' she asked.

'No.' And when she looked at him in surprise at the brusque reply he smiled most unfairly, so that she knew that she didn't want any time to think it over; she was going to accept his offer and never mind the consequences.

'The hours are quite good,' he explained, for all the world as though she had already accepted. 'Half past eight until one o'clock and Sunday free. It is about four kilometres away—ten minutes in Charlie, or if you prefer, you might borrow a bicycle.' He mentioned the money she would get and she nodded. A quite sufficient sum; she didn't spend all that much, it would keep her going while she took her time deciding what she was going to do, but while she was thinking that she knew in her heart that there was really only one thing possible; that was to go back to England the moment he married Loes. She hadn't her aunt's courage or patience, she reflected sadly; besides, he didn't need her, and his uncle had needed Aunt Henrietta.

'Well?' Marnix's voice broke in on her thoughts sharply, 'is it so difficult? You're standing there mooning when all you have to do is to say yes.'

She realized she was very cold. 'Yes,' she said shortly, adding: 'I'm frozen—how very like you to keep me standing here in this beastly wind.'

He grinned. 'Don't pretend that you're anything but tough, my girl,' he advised her, 'if you're so cold, why not come with me? I'm on my way over to Dominee Rietveld's house.'

The last place where she wanted to be, especially with him. She invented an on-the-spur-of-the-moment excuse, bade him a polite good-bye and sped across the square, wondering why he was going there—to see Loes, of course, she knew that already, but why? Perhaps he was going to ask her to marry him. Well, she would know soon enough; the village would know; probably, she thought bitterly, they would hang out flags.

There was nothing on the stove boiling over, of course; she had said the first thing to enter her head. She sat down in the dining-room without so much as removing her coat or gloves and with her scarf still tied under her chin, fighting dejection. She only half heard the front door open. She had left it on the latch because it was the day for Willemse to call; she didn't even bother to look up, not until Marnix went past her into the kitchen.

'Nothing boiling on the stove,' he remarked to no one in particular, 'and why are you sitting there in your outdoor clothes, Miss Brodie? and you were in such a hurry to get home.'

She eyed him peevishly and said crossly: 'I was cold,' then added even more crossly: 'How sick

and tired I am of you calling me Miss Brodie!' and
then: 'You were going to the *dominee*'s house...'

He was pulling her gloves from her hands in a
gentle fashion. 'That's right, to tell him the date of
the next meeting of Church Elders—it took me
about a minute.' He looked up suddenly, his grey
eyes very bright. 'I have my reasons for calling
you Miss Brodie.'

And what reasons might they be? She dismissed
that for the time being; his darling Loes hadn't
been home, then. She began to unbutton her coat
and was startled when he asked: 'Coffee?' in the
mildest of voices and before she could reply went
back to the kitchen; he must think her a poor hostess. She took off her coat and scarf and followed
him, to find the kettle already on the stove and the
coffee ground and ready to be filtered. She got two
mugs and put them on a tray and when he told her
to go and sit by the stove, she did so; after all, she
hadn't invited him and if he wanted to make the
coffee, it was all one to her. She picked up Henry
from his tea cosy and settled him on her knee; his
small whiskered face was soothing to her frayed
feelings so that when Marnix came in a few
minutes later with the tray, she felt quite amiable
again. 'This home for old people,' she asked, 'who
runs it? Is there a doctor and what happens when
they are ill?'

He had tossed his coat over a chair in a most

careless fashion before he sat down. 'There is a Matron, of course, and a number of staff—if any of the old people get ill they are nursed in the small hospital wing. There is a doctor too. The old people have their own flats, single or double, and their own furniture. They have their meals in the dining-room, but should they prefer it or they don't feel well enough, then they are served in their rooms. They have electric kettles and so on so that they can make their tea or coffee if they want to and each of them has a little shower room and all the help they need. I believe they are very happy.'

'Don't you have geriatric wards in Holland?'

'Oh yes, but the homes for the elderly far out-number them; only the really infirm go to the hospitals. It works very well; when an elderly couple get really past it and need home help and so on, or become a drag on their families, they may apply for a flat in one of these homes and if and when one is vacant, they move in with as many of their possessions as they can accommodate. They have to give up their pensions, of course, but they have pocket money each week and no worries of any sort as well as security, knowing that they will be allowed to stay together and whichever one is left will be cared for.' He put down his mug. 'If you can spare the time I'll come back in half an hour and take you over to see the place.'

'When do they want me to begin?' she wanted

to know, and was surprised when he said easily: 'Tomorrow, if you have a mind to do so.'

At the door she remembered to ask him: 'Who runs this place—you didn't say.'

He smiled down at her. 'I do,' he said.

He was back well within the time he had suggested. Henrietta was peeling vegetables for her dinner when he walked in again, and when she would have washed her hands and gone to get her coat, he told her to finish what she was doing in such a friendly voice that she turned back to her carrots and turnips. As she popped them into the pan already simmering on the stove, he asked: 'Stew?' and when she nodded: 'Is it not lonely living here by yourself?'

She was on her way to the stairs. 'You forget,' she told him soberly, 'that I am used to being by myself. Besides, I'm not alone, I have Henry.'

He had followed her and she was halfway upstairs when he spoke again. 'Have you no wish to marry, Henrietta?'

She paused with her back to him. 'Well, I get ideas about it, I suppose, like most girls—perhaps I expect too much...'

'Or dream too much. You are a girl who builds castles in Spain.' He sounded amused.

'No. I have a castle already,' she had forgotten for the moment to whom she was speaking, 'and it's not in Spain.' She saw it in her mind's eye,

solid and square, its white walls rising out of the
steely water and its funny clown's roof, and no
other castle would do—it was every dream castle
rolled into one, only it wasn't for her.

She was surprised to find Charlie in the street
outside. 'Ah, yes,' explained Marnix smoothly, 'I
thought it would be a good idea if you were to
drive—so that you know the road.' He had eased
his vast person into the seat beside her and handed
her the keys. 'You left these with Jan, I believe.
He's been doing a few little jobs, he's taken quite
a fancy to Charlie. Now, go across the square past
Dominee Rietveld's house and then carry straight
on until you come to the farmhouse on the left;
take the turning after that.'

She did as he had told her, resisting a desire to
slow down outside the *dominee*'s home, so that if
Loes were there, she would have a chance to see
them. It was a short drive, even in Charlie; the
Rusthuis was on the edge of the village, a modern
building softened by what, in summer, would be a
pretty garden. She pulled up neatly outside its entrance and he commented, 'You drive well,' a remark which needed no reply, as they went inside
together. The entrance hall was a pleasant place,
with bright wallpaper and handsome colourful pictures. There were chairs and tables here and there
too, but she was given no time to look around her
as she was whisked into a small room tucked away

behind a veritable bower of indoor plants. She found herself face to face with an elderly woman, very thin and severe-looking, although when she smiled the severity disappeared. She and Marnix had a quiet exchange in their own language before he introduced them and Henrietta, delighted to be given the chance to air her Dutch, said: '*Aangenaam, Mevrouw,*' and added ingenuously, 'I'm afraid that's about all I can say,' this time in English.

The severe lady laughed. 'But you said it very nicely,' she said in English. 'I am sure that you will manage very well and we shall be very glad to have your help, Miss Brodie. I hear that you are willing to start tomorrow, that is good news indeed.'

Henrietta turned a speaking eye upon the Jonkheer. 'I didn't know that I had said I would start tomorrow.'

The meekness of his expression was unbelievable. 'Oh, I must beg your pardon for anticipating your answer, my good—er—Henrietta. You see, I have already had proof of your kind heart and I knew that you would agree.'

She would have liked to have argued the point, but what was the use with a third party, all interested ears, there as well. She allowed herself a small indignant snort and turned back to the lady behind the desk. 'I'll be glad to help, but only on a temporary basis, please, so that I can leave when I want to.'

She saw that half of this speech hadn't been understood and waited while Marnix turned it into Dutch. The severe face lost its look of puzzlement and smiled again as she nodded and Marnix said: 'That is quite acceptable. Mevrouw Smit will allow you to leave whenever you wish. By the way, you should call her Directrice.'

She gave him a cold look. 'Thank you. How well you've arranged things. And what do I call you—Director?'

'How about Marnix?'

'Certainly not.' For a man who was all but engaged to be married he was showing a flippancy which she was discovering played havoc with her good intentions to keep him at a distance. They spent the rest of the visit discussing the details of her new job and visiting one or two of the old people, and she thought she had done rather well in getting their relationship on a more distant basis until she clashed her gears as they drove back and he observed on a sigh: 'Oh, my dear girl, who taught you to drive? You're far too impetuous— smoothness is essential, I believe I must give you some lessons.' A remark which made her heart leap with treacherous delight, although she asked him acidly if he wished her to stop so that he might get out and walk the rest of the way.

'No, no—I'm made of sterner stuff,' he told her, 'but since you are so touchy you might drop me off at the Rietvelds'—I daresay Loes will be back by now.'

Henrietta had nothing to say to that; she pulled up with an abruptness which did Charlie no good at all and waited silently while her companion un-wound himself from his cramped seat, and still si-lent, nodded briefly when he wished her good-bye in the friendliest voice imaginable, and then shot off across the square, narrowly missing the cat from the shop and grazing the little car's paintwork against one of the gateposts on her way into the castle grounds. That they were wide enough to take three Charlies abreast made it much worse.

The remainder of the day, as far as she was con-cerned, was a dead loss.

She got up early the next morning, glad to do so, for she had slept badly, did her chores, saw to Henry's wants and went to get the car. Jan was already there and Charlie was out of the garage, waiting for her. She drove carefully this time, Jan's mild observation that there was a nasty scratch on one wing ringing in her ears.

It was a dark morning and the lighted windows looked cheerful as she passed them; they made the road, once she had left them behind, seem even darker than it really was. But the Rusthuis was already lighted. Henrietta parked the car and went in, first to report for duty, then to collect her white overall and be told where to go: the top floor, to help with breakfasts, clear them away and then help such of the elderlies who needed it.

The morning flew by while she laced old-fashioned shoes, buttoned cuffs and combed hair into a variety of styles. She had been worried that she would have difficulty with the language, but surprisingly that was not so; she knew a great number of words by now and the old people, once they realized that she had a very good idea of what she was about, were content to smile and nod and point. She had the opportunity to air her Dutch during the coffee break too, for with the exception of the Directrice, no one else knew more than a few words of English. Henrietta, floundering happily in a hopeless mess of Dutch grammar, enjoyed herself.

She went back home to her dinner quite pleased with her first morning's work and was happily crashing her way through one of Chopin's Etudes with rather more feeling than technique, when she was interrupted by a knock on the door, and because the music had coloured her thoughts in an unreal fashion and she was thinking, almost unawares of Marnix, she went to the door with the absurd idea that it would be he. It wasn't—it was Loes, and Henrietta had the greatest difficulty in keeping the smile on her face. Loes was looking

charming and as guileless as a small child, and
Henrietta eyed her narrowly while she uttered all
the usual polite phrases and wondered silently why
she had come. She wasn't kept in the dark for long;
her visitor went through to the sitting-room with
every appearance of pleasure and had barely settled
herself before she began: 'I wanted to come and
see you, to know how you got on. I am glad that
Marnix took my advice and found work for you—
he has been concerned that you did not have
money, you see.' She smiled at Henrietta with a
quite sickening smugness. 'I indicated to him that
he must look after you just as he looks after the
people of the village.'

She sat back in her chair, looking like Lady
Bountiful; just as though, thought Henrietta, almost
choked with rage, she was already Marnix's
wife—and a horrible wife she would make too,
patronizing everyone, and what would he have to
say about it? She got to her feet, her temper now
under control, for the moment at any rate, though
she doubted if it would stay that way. She said in
a quiet voice: 'You know, Loes, I think you should
go. I don't like you and you don't like me; fur-
thermore I don't care for spiteful remarks, nor for
patronage. I think that if Marnix...' she saw the
girl's eyes flash at her use of his name, 'knew that
you had come here to—to gloat over me, he would
have something quite nasty to say; he would prob-

ably pin your ears back for you as well. You are not yet his wife, you know—and I very much doubt if you ever will be if you intend to go around throwing your weight about in the village—people don't like it. And I should be careful that your innocent little girl act doesn't turn sour on you, for if he gets just one glimpse of the real you, it will be curtains, ducky.' She paused for breath, quite pleased to get it all off her chest. 'You had a close shave on the afternoon of the plane crash, didn't you?' She nodded at her companion, hopelessly caught up in 'curtains' and 'turning sour' and 'ears'.

Loes muttered now: 'I do not understand you at all—what is this curtains and pinned ears and...'

'I should have thought it would have been plain in any language. Go home, Loes, and puzzle it out for yourself.'

Henrietta ushered her unwelcome guest, willynilly, to the door and flung it wide. Jonkheer van Hessel was outside, his hand raised to the knocker, and she shot him such a turbulent glance that his eyebrows lifted, although all he said was: 'I called to see how you got on today...' His gaze took in Loes and he smiled. 'Ah, Loes, I am glad to see that you are getting to know each other.'

'Oh, we know each other very well,' Henrietta told him snappishly. She looked at Loes. 'Don't let me keep you, I know you're anxious to be gone.'

The girl looked daggers, remembered that Marnix was watching and summoned up a smile as she muttered a brief good-bye and hurried away. 'Come in,' said Henrietta, her eyes still on the girl's back, unaware how beautiful she looked; her temper had given her a fine colour and her eyes sparked with rage, 'I want to talk to you.'

He made no move but stood staring down at her. 'Dear me,' his voice was blandly mocking, 'do I see signs of a nasty temper, my dear good girl? Why is that?'

'Come in and find out.' And when he did, without haste, she slammed the door behind him and brushed past him into the sitting-room. She had no very clear idea as to what she was going to say; she was hurt and surprised, and although she didn't quite believe all that Loes had said, there must be a grain of truth in it somewhere. She stood behind her chair, holding its back, facing him. 'How dare you?' she began, 'presuming to arrange my life for me just because it suited you to have extra help at the Rusthuis and telling Loes that I hadn't enough money—and then eyewashing me into thinking that there really was a job just because she suggested it, and how dare you,' she reiterated a shade too loudly and getting more and more muddled, 'allow her to practise being Lady of the Manor on me! She had no right—nor had you…patronizing me! You can have your job back again; when I

want work I'll find it for myself, I was never so...'
she gulped, 'I'm so angry!'

He was leaning against the door, watching her,
apparently unmoved by the inaccurate stream of
accusations, for all he said, and that mildly, was:
'Yes, I can see that, and now if you don't mind,
we'll start again from the beginning. I wouldn't
dare to arrange your life, my dear Miss Brodie,' he
smiled faintly as though at a little joke of his own,
'not at the moment at any rate. And I think that
perhaps Loes and you have misunderstood each
other; neither of you has a command of the other's
language. I have never discussed you with Loes,
nor would I ever do so, and I actually meant what
I said when I hoped that the job would enable you
to stay here for a longer period. You are, if I may
say so, remarkably touchy.'

'I am not!' Her voice had risen a little, she stared
at him haughtily, ignoring a weak desire to burst
into tears and cast herself into his arms. 'I am
merely curious to know why you should go to such
trouble to keep me here when you have shown
nothing but annoyance since the day I arrived. Naturally,' she went on inaccurately, 'I believed Loes.'

He was staring at her very hard. 'In that case,
Henrietta, I can hardly understand what all the fuss
is about, for even if you believed her when she
told you that I had offered you a job at her sug-

gestion—and you quite misunderstood her there— you could hardly consider that was going to a lot of trouble, could you? I would do the same service for any friend—or indeed, anyone.'

She all but ground her teeth at him. 'Don't be so beastly logical!' she flung at him, and he threw back his head and roared with laughter.

'Go away,' she begged, 'go away, do.'

'I believe I will, dear girl, but do, I beg of you, continue your work at the Rusthuis; the Directrice tells me that you were a great success this morning and there is no point in allowing the old people to suffer for one of your whims, is there?' With which parting shot he took himself off, leaving her to fling herself into a chair and recover her spirits as best she could.

But she didn't sit for long; being sorry for one-self got one nowhere, she had learned that years ago. She went upstairs and re-did her face and ti-died her hair, and a good thing too, because she had barely got downstairs again before someone plied the knocker again, and this time it was Mijn-heer van der Zande.

Because she was feeling so miserable herself Henrietta welcomed him with a warmth which caused him to smile broadly and say: 'You are pleased that I come, then? There is much I have to tell.'

'Tell away,' begged Henrietta, sitting him down

in the chair by the stove. 'Have you fixed things with your mother?'

'No, oh no—but I have seen Engelina and she would like very much to come and stay with you— is two days' time too soon?'

'Of course not. I've a job now, you know, but only in the mornings, if she wouldn't mind getting her own breakfast... I'll be home by one o'clock. I'd love to have her. Still a secret, is it?'

'Indeed yes, Miss Brodie. I think it will not be too difficult; you do not have many visitors, I think, and it is still dark very early in the evening and that is when I will visit.'

'Of course—better still, why not borrow my car? If anyone sees it they'll think it's me—you can bring it round from the garage or I could leave it outside when I come back from the Rusthuis and all you need to do is to get in and Engelina can join you. Simple.'

She beamed at him. 'I say, I can't go on calling you Mijnheer van der Zande, and I can't remember your name.'

'Pieter, Miss Brodie.'

'All right, Pieter, and for heaven's sake call me Henrietta.' She got up. 'Have a cup of tea? I was just going to make one.'

They drank their tea gossiping idly about the village and then once more discussed Engelina's visit. 'It's none of my business, of course, but had you thought of getting engaged and telling your mother after?'

He looked taken aback. 'Oh, Miss—Henrietta, that would be most dishonest! I do not think— besides, we are already *veloofde* and it is necessary that we should be *ondertrouwt* before we marry.'

'Goodness, don't you have special licences?' She saw the puzzled look on his face and added hastily: 'No, well, never mind that now. Can't you get—whatever it is and confront your mother with a *fait accompli*?'

'But it's almost marriage—it is binding...'

She felt she wasn't making much headway. 'Why not get Jonkheer van Hessel on your side? I'm sure your mother wouldn't raise objections if he were to approve of you marrying.'

'That is true. You are clever to think of these things, Henrietta, I do not know why you are not married.'

'I've often wondered that myself,' she answered dryly, 'but it's no good marrying someone you're not absolutely sure about, is it? You're sure of your Engelina, aren't you?'

'Yes,' he was reassuringly positive about that, 'it is only that I have no one to talk to about it and perhaps I am a little slow to do something even when I wish to do it very much.' He got to his feet. 'At what time shall Engelina come?'

'Oh, let me think. There's a bus stop where the

village road joins the motorway, isn't there? Could she come by bus in the evening and I'll pick her up there—the chance of anyone seeing us is almost nil—about six, I should think, when everyone will be indoors having their evening meal. Is there a bus then?'

'I think so. I will find out and let you know.'

She had opened the door and because he looked so uncertain and eager and very determined at the same time, she put a motherly hand on his arm. 'Don't worry, everything will turn out marvellously, you see if it doesn't.' She smiled at him and he smiled back, not seeing her at all, only his Engelina.

Neither of them saw the Jonkheer crossing the square in the thick darkness. He stopped and stood watching them, and it wasn't until she had closed the door that he walked on again, the darkness hiding his truly ferocious frown.

CHAPTER EIGHT

HENRIETTA was only just back from the Rusthuis the following day when Pieter called again, this time with an invitation from his mother to take tea with her that afternoon. 'And you will go, Henrietta?' he asked anxiously. 'She has been wanting to meet you...' His eyes beseeched her. Really, she thought with a touch of exasperation, he was a bit too meek; it was to be hoped that Engelina was made of sterner stuff, though somehow she doubted it.

'I'd like to come,' she said briskly. 'About three o'clock? Does your mother speak English, or do I have to do battle with my Dutch?'

'A few words only, I'm afraid, but I hear that your Dutch is really very good.'

'And who on earth would say anything so silly?'

'Jonkheer van Hessel is never silly,' she was reproved. 'He told me that listening to you speaking our language makes him realize how very difficult it is.' He delivered this doubtful compliment with the kindly smile of the expert encouraging the amateur. 'Moreover,' he went on, 'he is astonished that you can say so much without changing your tenses...'

Henrietta frowned. 'He made that up! He's never heard me speak Dutch.'

'Indeed he has, when the casualties from the crashed plane came to the castle—he listened to you with care,' she was assured.

'Then he must have ears like errant wings.'

He looked at her, puzzled. 'What is that—errant wings?'

'Oh, a bit of G. K. Chesterton.' She didn't say more. Pieter would be beside himself with annoyance if she mentioned that the bit was a particularly picturesque description of a donkey.

'Ah, yes—I have heard of him, of course. I must leave you, Henrietta, there is work for me to do on the other side of the estate, so I shall not be home when you visit my mother. You will not mind?'

She shook her head. 'Not at all. Is everything all settled with your Engelina?'

He nodded happily. 'Yes, she will wait at the bus station.' He added: 'You will not be late? It is cold in the evenings and she is not a robust woman as you are.'

Henrietta suppressed a giggle; she had never been called that before, it made her feel hearty and muscular and frightfully athletic, but she said soothingly, 'No, Pieter, I won't be late, and I'll take great care of her. You'll come round in the evening?'

'Yes. Mother goes to her sewing circle tomorrow evening—is that not fortunate?'

'Very. But, Pieter, you will have to rely on yourself, not fortune, you know.'

'I will, I promise you,' he said seriously, 'you see, I am an only son and my mother has depended on me since my father died—it is difficult.'

'Of course it is, but once it's all settled I'm sure she'll be glad to see you happily married—wait for the right moment, produce Engelina, and Bob's your uncle.'

His serious face became even more serious. 'I have no uncles.'

'Oh, lord—it's just an expression in English, it means everything will be all right.'

'Like OK?'

'Like OK.' She stood in the doorway and waved as he got into the Range Rover and drove away across the square, thinking how nice it would be if only she could tell Marnix all about it; he would know exactly what to do and the whole affair would be settled in hours, instead of days, perhaps weeks. She sighed and went to change her slacks and sweater for something rather more elegant for the afternoon's outing.

Pieter's house was on the boundary of the castle estate, and Henrietta, primed by him, walked through the village and reached it by a narrow lane outside the castle grounds. It stood by itself, a neat, unpretentious place with a nice little garden dividing it from the castle grounds, and although it appeared isolated it wasn't really, for she could see the solid back of the castle through the bare winter trees lining the drive which ran past the house. Five minutes' walk, no further, she calculated, and lovely in the summer—Pieter had a good job and a pleasant little home; there was no reason why he shouldn't stay there for the rest of his life with his Engelina. She rang the door bell and the door was opened so smartly that she concluded that Mevrouw van der Zande had been waiting for her on the other side of it—probably she had been watching her coming down the lane, too. She murmured her greetings in Dutch and offered a hand while she took stock of the lady, a tall, thin woman with a stern face which would look pleasant enough if it were allowed to relax into a smile. She was dressed soberly in black in a style which offered no concession to the current fashions, and her hair was drawn back in a no-nonsense manner, nor was there any make-up. A formidable lady and no mistake.

Henrietta, determined to get on her right side, smiled, excused her poor Dutch and was ushered into what was undoubtedly the best parlour. She had seen several of such rooms in the village, for while the younger Dutch housewives were as modern in their ideas as anywhere else in Europe, the older generation and the smaller villages stuck to their old ideas. A living-room used by all the family—comfortable and a little shabby, where they ate their meals and sat in the evenings, and the front room, its furniture kept in the pristine state in which it had been delivered from the stores, its lace mats and ornaments in their exact places, a handsome carpet on the floor, an important lamp-shade hanging from the ceiling...a room used for high days and holidays, for Sundays and visitors, weddings and funerals and christenings. Henrietta, casting a glance at the high gloss on the table before her, prudently put her handbag and gloves on the floor beside her chair and began the difficult task of conversation.

But not so difficult after all; Mevrouw van der Zande might not speak English, but she understood a good deal of it; after the first few awkward moments, they got on very well and presently, over the tea-cups, the elder lady began to talk about her son. That she was proud of him was obvious—his father had worked on the estate until his death; Pieter had studied hard to qualify for the same job. He was a good son, said his mother proudly.

'I'm sure he is,' said Henrietta in her ramshackle Dutch. 'Doesn't he plan to marry—then there would be a son to follow him.' She wasn't sure if she had made herself clear, but apparently her hostess had the gist of it, for she said: 'Pieter will not marry yet—he is not ready, only twenty-five, and that is far too young, and it must be to a girl who is worthy of him.'

'Someone Jonkheer van Hessel approves of?' asked Henrietta cunningly.

'Just so, Miss Brodie. If he should consider a young woman good enough for my son then naturally I should give my approval as well.'

'Naturally.' Henrietta spoke politely and thought: Feudal, oh, very feudal, it's like living in another world. But it was useful too; if she could get Marnix to give his blessing everyone was going to be satisfied; at least someone, she thought wistfully, would remember her with gratitude. It might be a good idea to change the subject before her hostess wondered why she was so interested. She accepted a second cup of weak, milkless tea and asked about the garden, and in a short time took her leave.

She had plenty to think about for the rest of that day and she was busy enough getting the second bedroom ready for her visitor and doing her shopping, a leisurely business because there was always someone there willing to let her try out her Dutch. It was only at bedtime that she allowed herself to think about Marnix, and then only briefly, and there was nothing sensible about her thoughts; she had forgotten all about Pieter and Engelina; she brooded over his bad temper, his good looks and the way he laughed suddenly, like a boy, and the way he had kissed her. She was still remembering that when she fell asleep.

It was raining and dismal when she reached the Rusthuis the next morning, but it was cosy enough inside and she was kept busy for the entire morning, doing all the small mundane tasks which were so necessary for the old people's comfort; it might not be very skilled work, but it was rewarding and satisfying. She drove back home, feeling more cheerful, and treated Henry to a detailed account of her morning's activities while she got their dinners.

She got to the bus station with ten minutes to spare that evening, and because it was so dark and miserable still, she got out of the car and went into the small café and had a cup of coffee. It was a cheerful little place and very clean; one of the things she liked about Holland, for almost all the bus stations had one as well as a telephone and a waiting room, all under one roof, so that waiting for a bus wasn't a miserable queue, shivering in the wind. The bus came in on time, paused long enough to disgorge one passenger from its crowded interior, take on several more, and disappear smoothly into the dark. Henrietta left her coffee and went up to the girl who had got out of the bus.

'Engelina, isn't it? I'm Henrietta Brodie. The car's over here.'

The girl, at first sight, looked a little like Loes, small and fair and pretty, but the blue eyes which smiled into hers were without guile, and the mouth was gentle above a small round chin which, she saw with regret, lacked firmness. But it was a dear little face; she could see why Pieter found it enchanting and wanted to marry its owner. She was exactly right for him, and his mother must be made to see that at all cost. They shook hands and Engelina said in a soft voice: 'I am glad to meet you, Miss Brodie—Pieter has been so clever to arrange this and it is very kind of you to help.' She spoke in English, slowly but well enough; Henrietta, who had been counting on practising her Dutch on her guest, gave up the idea; it would be far better to improve Engelina's English so that she could impress her future mother-in-law.

They got into the car and drove to Gijzelmortel, not saying much. The square was deserted, and Henrietta, feeling like a conspirator, got out first and opened the door so that Engelina could nip in quickly, and once in the lighted sitting room the two girls took stock of each other and after a moment smiled, pleased with each other. Engelina was nice, young and a little scared at her daring, but honest-eyed and quite prepared to do whatever Pieter decided was good for her. Henrietta, feeling positively motherly towards her, led her upstairs to her room and then went to the kitchen to get their supper. They had barely finished their gay little meal when Pieter arrived and Henrietta retired discreetly to the kitchen to make the coffee, wash up and feed Henry. It was half an hour before she judged that she might go back into the sitting room; the pair of them had had time to get over their first transports and there were one or two things to settle.

They turned round to look at her as she went in with the coffee tray, reminding her forcibly of two trusting children expecting help. It made her feel old, a fancy she instantly dismissed. 'Coffee,' she invited them, 'and have you made any plans?'

Pieter shook his head. 'You did mean it when you said that I might use your car and take Engelina for a drive?'

'Of course I meant it. Would you like it now? It's a beastly night, but I don't suppose you would have noticed that, and there's no one to see you.'

He looked at his watch. 'Mother gets back at ten o'clock. We will return in good time and I can take your car back to the garage before I go home. Is that suitable to you, Miss B...Henrietta?'

'Very suitable.' She would have to do something about Pieter's English too; he was such an earnest young man, prone to use long words when short ones would do, and yet he must be good at his job, or Marnix would never have kept him.

She saw them out of the door and went back to

the sitting room; she would have a pleasant hour or so with her tapestry work. She persevered with it, hating every stitch but not putting it down, for it kept her thoughts busy as well as her fingers. It was a relief when the others returned, looking pleased with themselves, though when she asked hopefully if they had made any plans, it was obvious from their answers that they hadn't. Pieter went almost at once, and Henrietta, peeping from the window with the light out, saw him start Charlie and drive away. By craning her neck she could see him as far as the castle gates, where he was forced to stop to allow the Rolls, coming from the other side of the square, to go through first. It worried her a little, the gates were well lighted, Marnix would have seen Charlie; there was no mistaking the little car, but possibly he hadn't seen who was driving it. If he had thought about it at all, he might have supposed that she had been out for the evening. She said nothing to Engelina, for it would only have disturbed her happy frame of mind, and presently they went up to bed.

Henrietta got up early, breakfasted, tidied the sitting room and took a cup of tea up to her guest, then with the advice not to open the door to anyone, took herself off to work. The morning was more than half done and she was helping an old lady to walk to the dining room for her dinner when Marnix van Hessel, coming silently behind them, brought them to a halt.

'Hullo,' said Henrietta, twisting her head round to see who it was, and quite forgetting that they had hardly parted the best of friends, she amended this to a sedate, 'Good morning, sir—did you want the Directrice?' and looked up into his face, and a very ill-tempered face it was too; there would be no good morning, then—but there never was. She wedged the old lady securely against her shoulder and waited patiently.

'I saw your car yesterday evening.' His voice was as bad-tempered as his face; it was obvious that only the truth would do—any little digressions from the facts would be pounced upon, worried like bones and handed back to her. She said brightly: 'Pieter van der Zande drove it round to the garage for me.'

'You had been out with him?'

She raised her brows a very little. 'No,' she told him evenly, 'he came to see me. I had left Charlie outside when I came back from work and he kindly offered to take it to the garage. Is there anything else you want to know?' Her voice was very sweet. 'I can't think what business it is of yours, unless we have to ask permission to visit...?'

She peeped at him as she spoke, her eyes wide, their lashes fluttering most fetchingly. His face was thunderous, so she said prudently: 'No, don't answer that, you're in a fearful temper and I won't have this nice old thing frightened out of her wits. And now if you haven't any more questions, we'll trundle on; there's quite a long way to go and we mustn't let her dinner get cold.'

His eyes were half closed so that she missed the gleam in them, indeed she didn't look at him at all, but hoisted up the old lady and started off again in the direction of the dining room. She longed to look back and see if he was still there, but that would never do; besides, the old lady might fall over if she did.

She told Pieter about it when he came that evening. 'Do you suppose it would be better if you didn't use the car?' she wondered out loud. She nibbled a well manicured finger, deep in thought. 'I don't see why not, though—if anyone should see you go out they'll only think it's you and me, won't they? And it's most unlikely that you'll be seen; it was just bad luck last night, but no harm done.'

So the two of them drank their coffee with her, and then, holding hands like two children, went out to the car. They were seen by Loes, on her way to the castle to return a book she had borrowed from Marnix—it was amazing, for a girl who read almost nothing but magazines, how her interest had suddenly blossomed to embrace the learned volumes he lent her. She stood in the dark, watching the two figures getting into the car and drive away, and only when they were quite out of sight did she resume her journey; there had been no chance of them having seen her, but she was a girl who took precautions.

She hadn't decided whether to tell Marnix when she saw him; she was half inclined to keep quiet about it until the right moment, but she was piqued by his coolness towards her; he responded to none of her deliberate little wiles in order to gain his attention, and worse, he had made no attempt to kiss her, merely offering her another book before pleading a mass of work and escorting her to the castle door. Half-way across the hall, however, spite got the better of prudence and she told him that she had seen Miss Brodie and Pieter van der Zande go out together not half an hour earlier, and her initial disappointment at his complete lack of interest in her news was tempered presently by the thought that whether he was interested in the English girl or not—and she had a growing suspicion that he was—she had sown a seed of doubt in his mind.

There was no reason why Henrietta shouldn't go out if she wished, of course, but if Marnix was developing a fondness for her, he wouldn't like it; Pieter, thought Loes with a perception she seldom used, was a young man; Marnix was forty. She stared at her pretty face in her bedroom mirror and nodded and smiled to it. She would keep a sharp eye open, she promised herself. The next morning she told old Mevrouw Tinte, who came to clean the house each day—in the strictest confidence, of course, knowing that by the end of the day, most of the village would have been told; Mevrouw Tinte was the greatest gossip for miles around.

Henrietta, happily unaware of this, spent her morning with the old people, her afternoon improving her guest's English and when the evening came, since it was a wet one she retired tactfully to the dining room to write letters, leaving her two protégés in the sitting room. She hoped that they would spend the time in deciding about their future, and if by the time Pieter went home, they hadn't hit on something, she decided that she would suggest that she went to Marnix and asked his advice. She was loath to do this, for he would probably tell her to mind her own business; it would be much better if Pieter had a talk with him.

She put the idea to them later and Pieter promised gravely that he would think the matter over carefully and tell her what he had decided. She would have liked him to have shown a little more dash and verve, but he wasn't like that and it was going to take time. She went into the kitchen while they said good night and then saw him out of the front door; several of the more inquisitive neighbours saw them quite clearly, and Willemse the greengrocer, putting his van away for the night, had a really splendid view, as he told Klara in the castle kitchen a short time afterwards. He was a little worried about it; he had heard rumours and discounted them as gossip; it was a small village and the things that happened in it sometimes got exaggerated, but now he had seen them with his own eyes. 'And it's not just this evening,' he assured Klara, 'only I never believed them...'

Klara shrugged her shoulders. 'Gossip,' she declared. 'Probably Mijnheer van der Zande has business with Miss Brodie—such a nice young lady. It will have to be repeated a great many times before I listen to talk of that sort about her.'

It was unfortunate that Marnix himself saw his agent going into Henrietta's house the very next evening, it reminded him of what Loes had told him and caused him to enter his home in a black rage which sent him to his study with the curt order that he was not to be disturbed, and when an hour or so later he demanded his agent's presence, he was told that that gentleman had been seen leaving the castle grounds in Miss Brodie's car. A piece of information which inflamed him into the exact mood required by Loes, who had called on some excuse or other to see Jonkvrouw van Hessel, and had spun out her visit in the hope that he might join them in the drawing room. She was far too clever to ask why he looked so furiously angry but talked prettily about nothing in particular for a few minutes before mentioning, ever so casually, Henrietta's work at the Rusthuis; from there it was an easy step to a mild observation on the frequent visits of Pieter van der Zande to her house—it was done cleverly and then lightly dismissed with a vague laughing reference to village gossip. Loes left shortly after, accepting Marnix's offer to run her back with a wide-eyed smile which caused his mother to grit her teeth.

During their brief journey he was civil and nothing more, but Loes was too conceited a girl to see that he was in a cold rage. He left her at her door, refusing an invitation to go in with her and bidding her a good night which at best could be described as lukewarm.

He bore his mother company for the rest of the evening, answering her quiet remarks with punctilious politeness and maintaining between them a thoughtful silence which she forbore from commenting upon. If he hadn't been so occupied with his thoughts he might have observed the satisfied little smile upon his parent's face.

It was the following day, when Henrietta got back from the Rusthuis, that they discovered that the roof was leaking on the landing. She prudently put a bucket to catch the drips and setting about hunting down its source, saw quickly enough that it was beyond her powers to remedy it; one of the old bright red tiles had slipped; by peering closely from the back garden she could just make it out— a ladder, and preferably a man on it, would do the trick. And it would have to be put right soon; it had been raining all the morning and showed no sign of stopping. She left Engelina in the kitchen, rammed her feet back into her boots, dragged on her raincoat and headscarf once more and marched up to the castle. She was almost across the bridge when its door was flung open wide and Jonkheer van Hessel strode down to meet her.

'What now?' he bellowed, dispensing, as usual, with the formalities of greeting.

She stood in the pouring rain, looking down her beautiful nose at him and loving him with all her heart as well as disliking him heartily for his arrogance. She was cold and a little tired and not happy, and there had been no need to bellow at her like that. She said, thinking her thoughts out loud: 'You should have been born a couple of hundred years ago,' and then went on briskly: 'There is a leak in my roof. I have already filled one bucket and I daresay by the time I get back it will be filled again. Something must be done about it at once.' She cast a smouldering eye at the leaden skies. 'Your beastly Dutch weather,' she added irritably.

He had joined her on the bridge, not caring about the rain. 'My dear good woman, since you dislike our climate so much, why not return to your own country?'

His voice was cold and this sudden open acknowledgement of his dislike hurt dreadfully; all the same she made herself answer quietly: 'And let Aunt Henrietta's little house fall into a forgotten heap? Oh, no!'

He bent a kindling eye upon her, the rain running down his handsome face and dripping off his majestic nose. 'And what am I supposed to do about it, pray? Get a ladder and repair it for you?'

She ignored the sarcasm. 'No,' she told him reasonably, 'I'm sure you won't do that, but if you would tell me where you keep the ladders, I believe I could do it easily by myself.'

He stared at her in silence, then: 'Unthinkable, as you are well aware, Miss Brodie. I will send a man round at once and later today van der Zande shall come and inspect it. You will like that, I daresay?'

She looked back at him, quite bewildered, not understanding him at all. At length she said in a soft voice: 'You're getting wet.'

'And whose fault's that?' he demanded nastily.

Such an unfair remark, and she had no idea how to answer it without making him even nastier, so she remained silent until, realizing that he had no intention of saying anything more, she said thank you in a subdued voice and turned round and marched over the bridge and down the drive. There was a man on the doorstep within minutes of her return; she just had time to tell Engelina to stay in the kitchen and not come out until she was told before he started his work. And later, after they had had their dinner, Pieter came. He was looking pleased with himself as she let him in, observing: 'Is it not lucky that I have a reason for coming? I am to inspect the work which has been done on your roof, Henrietta, and make sure that it is good.'

She led the way into the sitting room. 'Have you said anything to Jonkheer van Hessel?' she demanded, barely giving him time to greet Engelina.

'Unfortunately, not. He is today—how do you say it?—suffering from an irritation of the spirits which makes it difficult to approach him about anything but business connected with the estate.'

'Oh, lord,' said Henrietta impatiently. 'Look, I'll tackle him—not today, though; I couldn't agree more about the irritated spirits—tomorrow afternoon when I get back from work—that's if he will be home?' She looked at Pieter. 'It'll be Wednesday, isn't that his morning at Tilburg and nothing else?'

'Yes, that is so,' he answered her promptly, but his eyes were on Engelina; plainly she wasn't going to get much help from either of them. It was extraordinary that Pieter, so efficient in his work, could be so helpless when it came to arranging his own life. After all, he only had to go to Marnix and talk to him about it—she remembered her own reception that morning and had to admit that anyone less likely to lend a sympathetic ear to his agent's little problems would be hard to find. With herself, it didn't really matter how rude he was, just as long as he listened long enough to understand that a word in Mevrouw van der Zande's ear would set the ball rolling, as it were, to the altar.

She sighed and then smiled quickly because they were both looking at her. 'It will be all right, I'm sure of that,' she assured them cheerfully. 'I'll go up to the castle and it will be sorted out in no time.'

She couldn't have been more wrong; for although she went to the castle the next day, just as she had said, nothing was sorted out; indeed, she had said nothing of what she wanted to say, and a great many things she had never intended to utter. It had gone wrong from the start; she had been ushered into his study and found him at his desk, deep in papers, and because the telephone rang as she entered the room, she was forced to take the chair he waved her to and sit silent for upwards of a minute while he carried on a conversation. And when he did put the receiver down he greeted her with: 'Well, another leak?' in the nastiest voice imaginable.

She had resolved to keep her temper at all costs, but the look from his grey eyes made her forget that. 'No. I've come upon an entirely personal matter—at least, it concerns someone else as well.'

His face became very still. 'Yes? Pieter van der Zande, perhaps?'

She smiled her relief. 'Oh, yes,' and then with sudden apprehension, 'How did you know? We've been so careful…'

His smile made her shiver. 'Indeed you have, Miss Brodie, and I cannot think why; surely you must know that the more careful you are in a village the more likely you are to be discovered? Each time van der Zande calls at your house and each time you leave it with him, you are seen by someone or other. Indeed, I have myself seen you both.'

She goggled at him. 'Seen me?' she repeated uncertainly, her mind in a fine state of confusion.

'Close your mouth, Miss Brodie, you look like a stranded fish—and there is no need to act in such a surprised fashion. Do you really believe that I am blind and deaf? Oh, I don't listen to gossip, but when I am told the same tale by several people—even Loes—oh, yes, she has seen you too, although it was mere chance that she mentioned it to me.'

I bet it was, fumed Henrietta silently. She said icily: 'And of course you believed everything you heard, especially when Loes…' she paused; there was no point in being catty, he would merely think even worse of her. Her lovely eyes narrowed. 'And now we're on the subject perhaps you will tell me exactly what you have heard? I have a right to know.' She made a small indignant snorting noise and he said softly:

'I advise you to keep your temper, Miss Brodie. Certainly you have a right to know, but isn't it rather a silly question? You must surely realize that if you wish to—er—carry on is perhaps the kindest way of putting it—with young Pieter, you must be prepared to be in the village limelight? We are a god-fearing people here, and very old-fashioned. We conduct our courting in the light of day.'

She was on her feet. 'You big pompous…you—you despot…how dare you…' she was stuttering with temper. 'Anyone would think that you owned the people as well as the village! Well, all I can say is you deserve Loes for a wife!'

She flounced to the door and her hand was on its handle when he said quietly: 'What a pity that I shan't get my deserts; I have no intention of marrying—not now.' He got up and crossed the room and took the handle out of her grasp. 'It is a very great pity.' His voice was gentle, almost sad as he opened the door and pushed her through carefully and closed it soundlessly behind her.

Pieter came that evening, and she poured out the whole story to him and Engelina. 'So you see,' she

said finally, 'I've made a mess of it—now you will
have to do something, Pieter.'

He was annoyingly cheerful. 'But of course,
Henrietta. It is only an amusing mistake that Jonkheer van Hessel thinks that I come here to visit
you,' he paused to laugh, 'for of course he knows
nothing about Engelina.' He looked at her inquiringly. 'Why did you not tell him?'

'Me? Tell him? After all the beastly things he
said—I'd rather have died!' She lifted her chin. 'I
never want to talk to the man again!' On which
mendacious note she went up to bed and left the
two of them.

She lay awake a long time wondering what to
do; she couldn't say anything to Loes, not until
Pieter had revealed Engelina's whereabouts, and
that was a pity, because there were a number of
things she would have liked to have said to that
young lady. She couldn't go to Jonkvrouw van
Hessel, for there was no reason to suppose that she
was in the least interested, and it was hopeless to
talk to the two downstairs. But later, she promised
herself, when the muddle had been cleared up, she
would extort an apology from Marnix, after which
she would never speak to him again. This resolution, which should have satisfied her, served to
keep her awake for the rest of the long night.

She met Loes the following afternoon on her
way back from the butcher's van and, quite for-

getful of her decision to say nothing to her, stopped squarely in front of her. 'And just what did you see the other evening?' she asked in a voice which shook just a little with her rage. 'And I'll stake my life that it was you who started those silly stories about Pieter van der Zande and me!'

Loes gave her a scared look. 'What if I did?' she answered defiantly. 'I wish you to go from here, Miss Brodie, and now there is a reason for you to go, is there not? All this gossip is not nice, eh?' Angry tears sprang to her eyes. 'Marnix has never looked at any other girl for weeks, and then you come, and you are not even young any more. I hate you, and I wish that he would hate you too, and you will see that he will. It is so simple for I am clever with him; I say so very little, you see, a word here, a word there, and in a little while he will wish to have nothing more to do with you— so you may as well go now, although,' she added thoughtfully, 'I would like you to come to our wedding—to see us married.'

Henrietta turned on her heel and walked away; the girl was dreadful and Marnix deserved her. She shuddered at the idea of him living for the rest of his life with Loes, and then told herself that her pity was wasted. She went indoors and drank the tea Engelina had made for them both and talked cheerfully about Pieter and how wonderful he was, while her heart became heavier and heavier. If only he would pluck up courage!

He had. He had finished his day's work and had gone to the study to lay the estate books before his employer, and half-way through their perusal, he had suddenly found his voice. The whole story poured out, not the haphazard muddle which Henrietta might have disclosed, but well phrased, the arguments in their right order, the sequence of events clearly stated. Marnix had laid down his pen and was sitting back in his chair, listening silently. When his agent had at last finished, apologizing for taking up his employer's valuable time and reiterating his deep love for Engelina and his determination to marry her whether his mother liked it or not, his listener asked merely: 'And Miss Brodie? what does she think?'

Pieter looked surprised. 'Why, she thinks that we should marry, *mijnheer*. That is why she helped us—it is she who thought that you should be told so that you might speak to my mother; if you were to approve of Engelina then my mother would also.'

'And that is what Miss Brodie came to see me about? She told you of our conversation?'

Pieter looked uncomfortable. 'A mistake, *mijnheer*, and so easily made. She was upset and for some reason she did not wish to tell you…'

The big man sitting so relaxed in his chair smiled across the desk at him. 'No. Bring Engelina to see me this evening,' he went on, 'and we will discuss what may be done. Your mother must not be made unhappy, but I should prefer you to be married, Pieter, and perhaps I can convince her of the suitability of this.' He nodded kindly and picked up the books again. 'About eight o'clock, then.'

Henrietta got to her feet, made the coffee and urged her
guests to eat, more so that they might make the most
of it than through further, useless argument with her
suitors.

After this the evening went quickly. It was dawn before
her mother, asleep over her knitting, woke when their last

CHAPTER NINE

HENRIETTA opened the door to a changed Pieter,
an excited young man who strode resolutely past
her to embrace his Engelina and then break into a
stream of Dutch. She shut the door, edged past
them and went to sit in her chair with Henry on
her lap until such time as they should come to their
senses. Something momentous had happened, that
much was obvious; she was glad of it and turned
an expectantly smiling face towards them as they
joined her, both talking at once, Engelina's slow
schoolgirl English standing no chance at all against
Pieter's correct pedantic phrases. But Henrietta
was an intelligent girl; by listening closely and
popping in a leading question here and there she
made sense of the chorus and when they paused
for breath exclaimed: 'Oh, Pieter, how very clever
of you!' She watched his face as she spoke. He
had taken a long time to get going, but now, with
some support from Marnix, he would go ahead and
get married, and his mother, provided she were
dealt with tactfully would turn out to be not the
bogey woman who had—lovingly no doubt—
smothered him and ruled his life, but an ordinary
loving mum. She kissed them both warmly, told

Pieter to go and make the coffee and urged Engelina up the stairs so that she might make the best of herself for the forthcoming interview with the Jonkheer.

After they had gone she went and sat down, doing nothing, going over in her mind what Pieter had told her. Apparently Marnix had been most helpful, but he had asked no questions, nor had he made any reference to his mistake in thinking it was she that Pieter had been visiting with such regular stealth. She wondered if he intended doing anything about it; an apology wouldn't come amiss, but however much he humbled himself— and that was unlikely, she told herself furiously— she would never forgive him. She would have nothing further to do with him; it would be a little difficult, for she would be bound to meet him from time to time in the village, but beyond the barest civilities there would be no need to speak to him. The idea almost brought tears to her eyes, but she blinked them away. She certainly wasn't going back to England even if that was what he wanted her to do. She remembered the episode of the leaking roof and sniffed away another lot of tears.

Whether he liked it or not she would attend his wedding in a smart new outfit and never mind the expense—she would show him... She began to plan it, quite carried away with the idea, and was surprised when Pieter and Engelina came bursting in. Everything had been wonderful, they told her. Jonkheer van Hessel approved of their marrying— indeed, he had complimented Pieter on his choice and told Engelina that she was a very pretty girl and would no doubt make a splendid wife. More-over, he had undertaken to go at once to talk to Mevrouw van der Zande and had then taken them to the drawing room to talk to his mother, who had offered them coffee. So fortunate, exclaimed En-gelina, getting in a word at all costs, that her dear Miss Brodie had advised her to wear the green vel-vet pinafore dress with the blouse…

Henrietta answered suitably, offered more cof-fee, and after they had drunk it, mindful of the possibility of Marnix taking the notion into his head to call and tell them the result of his visit, declared her intention of going out to post some letters. 'And I may,' she added with a complete disregard for the truth, 'go and see Dominee Riet-veld.' She could see from her hearers' faces that she might just as well have told them that she was off to the moon, for all the attention they paid her, and although they smiled and nodded as she went to fetch her coat, she was aware that they really had no idea of what she had said.

She dragged on her outdoor things anyhow; it was almost two hours since they had returned, time enough for Marnix to have paid his visit. Any min-ute now he might bang the door knocker. She should have gone sooner, she thought worriedly, for it would be most vexing to meet him. She opened the front door cautiously and peered round it. He was leaning against the side of the little house, his hands in his pockets, one long leg crossed over the other. He said genially:

'Ah, our thoughts run on similar lines, Miss Brodie—you are intent on escape before I get here, and I am determined to prevent you from doing so.' He smiled with charm. 'How well I timed it!'

She eyed him a trifle wildly. 'I'm going out,' she said, stating the obvious. 'I daresay you want to see Pieter and Engelina—they're in the sitting room.' She opened the door a few inches wider and slid round it into the street, but was instantly borne gently back into the hall again and he with her. He shut the door carefully and hustled her into the sitting room before she could so much as utter, and by the time she had found her tongue, it was too late, for he was talking.

'I've seen your mother,' he told Pieter, 'and we have had a talk. I believe that if you were both to go and see her now, you will find that everything has been smoothed out in a satisfactory manner. I have suggested several possibilities for her future once you are married, and there will be a small house for her very shortly if she cares to remain in the village—I think that she likes that idea.'

His agent eyed him worriedly. 'A house, *mijn-*

heer? I cannot recall that there are any houses vacant on the estate at this time.'

'I said very shortly. I should advise you to go at once.'

There was an instant putting on of coats and scarves, and when they were ready, Henrietta, still dressed to go out, said in a calm voice which seemed a miracle to her considering how she was shaking inside:

'I have to go out too. You are welcome to stay here until they return, Jonkheer van Hessel.'

She took a step towards the door and felt a large firm hand clamp itself round her waist. 'No, you don't. I want to talk to you.'

She had forgotten the other two, who had paused to stare. 'We have nothing to talk about,' she declared roundly. 'Kindly let me go!'

'No.' He caught his agent's eye and that young man took Engelina by the arm and hurried her away without a word or even a backward glance.

'Really,' said Henrietta, 'it is absurd the way people obey you—just as though you owned the place...'

'Well, I do,' he said reasonably. 'Henrietta, will you forgive me for believing that you were having an affair with van der Zande?'

'No, I won't! You had no reason to think anything so utterly stupid, and you had no right to speak to me as you did.'

'Yes, I did,' he said to surprise her, 'but this is hardly the moment to explain that. Later—when you have accepted my apology.'

'But I'm not going to accept it,' she told him crossly. 'I don't want to have anything more to do with you; we shall have to be civil when we meet, I suppose—and it doesn't matter how much you want me to go, I'm not going.'

'Now that is awkward,' his face was blandly cheerful. 'I thought that this house might do very well for Mevrouw van der Zande.'

She put a shaking hand up to her headscarf and pushed it back. 'You're not serious? But you can't—it's my house, my home. I'd never let you.'

'I am hoping to persuade you to my point of view.' He had cast off his coat and was sitting in one of the velvet chairs, very much at his ease. 'You only have to agree to let her have it, you know—it will be quite legal.'

'But what's to become of me?' She looked at him like a bewildered child.

'Ah, yes—well, I thought we might discuss that. I have something in mind...'

'No!' She spoke quite violently and picking up Henry, tea cosy and all, ran from the room and upstairs into her room, where she sat down on her bed, her mind, usually so sensible and active, a complete blank. After a minute or two good sense prevailed; it was no good giving way to him just because he expected her to. She put Henry carefully down on the bed, took off her coat and scarf, did things to her face and hair and went downstairs again. Marnix got up as she entered the room, smiling a little, his face so kind that she found it a little difficult to begin. 'I thought I must just tell you that I won't give up this house, and as well as that you're not welcome here, and if we have to meet at any time, I prefer not to speak to you.' She gave a sharp little nod and turned on her heel, to be halted by his voice, very quiet and gentle.

'I will respect your wishes, Miss Brodie, although I shall move heaven and earth to persuade you to leave this house—and that is a promise. I had thought...but no matter, in the circumstances I couldn't have expected otherwise. May I stay until those two get back so that the matter of their marriage may be settled once and for all?'

'Pray do.' She went back upstairs without looking at him.

Henrietta half expected that Engelina would come to her room when they got back presently, to tell her what had happened, but no one came. It wasn't until she went downstairs in the morning that Engelina followed her into the kitchen. 'Jonkheer van Hessel asked us to be quiet last night because you weren't feeling well—you are better, I hope? I wished very much to come and see you, but he said that I must wait until morning. Oh, Henrietta, it is all arranged, is it not pleasant? We are to be married in a few months and Pieter's mother says that I will be a good wife for her son because Jonkheer van Hessel says that too, and she is to remain in the village, and Pieter is to have more money so that we shall not be poor.' She hugged Henrietta, who made a great effort and displayed the delight suitable to the occasion.

'That's wonderful news,' she said cheerfully. 'Now Pieter can come and see you whenever he wants and there won't be any more silly stories going round the village.'

Engelina laughed. 'That was funny, I think and there will be no need for Pieter to come here. I have loved being here with you, but now I am to stay with Pieter's mother for a few days before I go home—there is so much to do, the wedding to arrange, and clothes.' She became lost in a happy dream for a few seconds. 'My parents will visit Mevrouw van der Zande, of course, and she will visit them—everything will be done correctly.'

'It sounds fun,' said Henrietta as she made the tea. She was dressed and about to go down to her breakfast when she heard the Rolls' telltale purr outside the house, and when Marnix thumped the knocker she didn't go down to answer it, but flung up the bedroom window, letting in a rush of icy air as she stuck her pretty head out. 'Go away,' she told him. His upturned face looked white and strained in the grey light, but when he said deliberately: 'Good morning, Henrietta. May I come in?' she hardened her unhappy heart. 'No, I will not open my door to you!' and for fear of weakening she slammed the window down again and presently she heard the Rolls whisper itself away. She had never felt so lonely.

The little house seemed very quiet after Engelina had left and Pieter didn't call any more. Henrietta flung herself into a bout of quite unnecessary cleaning, attacking cupboards and silver and furniture so that each day she went to bed tired out, to fall asleep and wake far too early. She had seen nothing more of Marnix; the castle stood, four-square and solid, silently dominating the village, and for all the signs of life there were, it could have been empty, and although when she went to fetch Charlie she found him cleaned and polished just as carefully as he always had been, there was no sign of Jan.

The only person she had spoken to, other than a brief excited visit from Engelina and her usual chatty encounters in the village shop, had been the *dominee*, who had stopped her as she crossed the square. He had surprised her very much by stopping; he had obviously been in a hurry to go home, yet he crossed the few yards between them and began at once to tell her that Loes had gone away.

'Rather suddenly,' he observed, 'or she would have let you know,' he smiled his mild innocent smile. 'She dislikes the winter, you know, and I have a sister living in the south of France, so Loes telephoned her on the spur of the moment and asked if she might go there until the warm weather returns. I had a letter from her this morning and she is delighted with everything; my sister has a large family, all about Loes's age—the poor child had little to amuse her here, I'm afraid, and I am pleased that she is so happy.'

Such a nice man—far too nice to have Loes for a daughter. 'And you,' she asked, 'can you manage alone?'

'Oh, dear me, yes; Mevrouw Tinte is only too glad to come each day and cook as well as do the housework. Loes was not a good cook, I am afraid.' He laughed gently and she laughed with him, commented suitably upon his news and went back home. So Loes had gone away, and why? Was it a ruse to get Marnix to go after her? Wasn't absence supposed to make the heart grow fonder? Or had they quarrelled? But surely Marnix would never have let her go like that—provided that he really wanted to marry her. Although he had said that evening at the castle that he had no intention of marrying—he had added 'not now', too. Perhaps they had already decided to part. She gave up thinking about it because there was still an hour of a surprisingly fine afternoon left and she could dig her little back garden. The exercise made her healthily tired so that she slept better than she had done for several nights.

She wakened early and found the fine weather still holding, and since there was no point in lying in bed, she got up, breakfasted and saw to Henry's small wants, wrapped up warmly and set out to walk to the Rusthuis. The early morning was chilly, but the country looked nice if a little bare under the wide sky. She arrived in a warm glow and set about her tasks, carrying on conversations with the old people while she dressed them and helped them toddle down to the sitting room; she was making progress with her Dutch at last, largely due to the help she received from those she worked with. She left after dishing out the dinners, glad of the fresh air after the cosy warmth of the dining room.

The sky had clouded over by now and it was a good deal colder. She glanced at the clouds curling up over the horizon and guessed that there would be snow before long; the winter seemed to be taking a long time, but it would be pleasant when the spring came. She would get out and about, she told herself, marching along at a fine pace, and began to plan all the things she would do when the days got longer—longer and emptier without the chance of seeing Marnix. She was going to find avoiding him difficult, but perhaps he would avoid her; the uneasy suspicion that he blamed her for Loes going away popped into the back of her mind and she was worrying about it without getting any nearer to its solution when she happened to glance across the fields to see how the clouds were getting on. They had come a good deal nearer and the flat water meadows on either side of the road looked drained of colour, but it wasn't the clouds which drew her attention, it was something lying in the grass, some distance off on the other side of a *sloot*. It was something large. Henrietta stopped the better to look and saw it trying to rear itself up and heard a faint whinny—a horse. She knew nothing about horses and this one, even at that distance, looked enormous. It also looked as though it might need help.

She slid down the bank at the side of the road, jumped the *sloot* and began to walk across the field. The horse was some way off; half-way there she turned to look back at the road in case there might be a passing car, but the likelihood of this was small; it was midwinter and dinner time, and the road, moreover, one which was seldom used. She hurried her pace; at least she could have a look and see what was the matter.

The beast was lying on its side, its eyes distended, its nostrils flared, and she saw with the first glance that it was trying to foal without success. It was a large animal; she had become used to the sight of the enormous horses the farmers still used; great powerful slow-moving beasts, well cared for, too. How this one came to be in its present predicament she had no idea, and now was not the time to waste in speculation. She had a closer look; it would need a man, and a skilled one at that, someone strong and knowledgeable, and even then if the foal was safely born, they would both need shelter and warmth. She looked round the fields and could see no buildings at all, although she remembered that down the road, round the next bend, there was a farm on the other side—she would have to run there as quickly as she could and get help, but first she went and knelt at the beast's head and told her what she was going to do. 'I'm terribly sorry,' she told the animal in English, just as though it could understand every word, 'but I can't think of anything else to do and there's no one about.'

She was wrong. Marnix van Hessel, driving the Range Rover towards the Rusthuis, had seen her and stopped to look more closely. He knew that she had walked to work; she would have been surprised to know that over the last few days he had made it his business to know just where she was and what she was doing, and now, with bad weather blowing up, he had started off to pick her up and drive her back home. She had said, quite definitely, that she never wanted to speak to him again and he hadn't forgotten that; if necessary he would toss her into the car and take her home— without speaking a word, of course. Now he stared across the meadows, driving again, but very slowly. His tiresome, proud Henrietta was having trouble of some sort, and so, unless he was very much mistaken, was the horse. He stopped the car, got his bag from the back, together with a length of rope, and in his turn strode down the bank and over the *sloot* towards the two figures in the distance.

Henrietta had taken the mare's head on to her knee because the poor beast was afraid now and she couldn't leave her in that state. She didn't hear Marnix's feet on the grass but some instinct made her turn her head.

She said at once, her whole face alight at the sight of him. 'Oh, Marnix, I'm so glad it's you!' She looked up at him with complete trust, confident that he would know just what to do. 'She's having a foal, only something's gone wrong and I don't know what to do—I was just telling her I would have to go for help...'

He nodded gravely, his eyes smiling, although he looked nothing more than friendly. He said in a placid voice: 'I'll have a look, shall I? Then perhaps we can manage something between us before getting help.'

He had taken off his coat and was rolling up his shirt sleeves.

'You'll catch your death of cold,' warned Henrietta.

'I daresay we all shall if this business isn't done with quickly—there's bad weather coming up fast.' He had got on his knees and was examining the mare, and went on without looking up: 'Stay where you are for the moment, will you? Soothe her as best you can and try and keep her still.'

He set to work, and Henrietta, cradling the great head on her cold knees, watched him. Marnix showed no signs of alarm or hurry and he seemed to know exactly what to do, although it took a long time. Long before the foal had been safely delivered, large, slow snowflakes were swirling round them and the sky had taken on a yellowish grey with no sign of a break in the clouds. The mare had lain quietly; now she was exhausted and Henrietta asked anxiously: 'Oh, dear, now what do we do?'

He was bending over the mare. 'I think we're in luck. I can hear something—a tractor, by the sound of it—coming down the road. Would you take off your headscarf and wave it? They might see it—I don't like to leave this animal for the moment, so if they miss us, I'm afraid you'll have to sprint after them.'

The scarf was seen; two men came across the

fields, received instructions from Marnix and hurried away again. 'There's a horse box at the farm,' he explained. 'They're going to fetch it and we'll load this pair in—the vet should be out by then to see them both—I doubt if they take much harm.'

'Who owns the poor beast?'

'Van Tiel. They tell me he went to market this morning—the mare wasn't due to foal for another two weeks.' He looked across the heaving flanks and smiled at her. 'Don't worry, he's good to his animals. I wouldn't have a farmer on my land who wasn't.' He turned his attention to the foal once more and left her to her thoughts, interrupted presently by the arrival of the horse box, the same two men and two more besides.

There was a great deal of heaving and shoving, accompanied by encouraging cries from the men and some indignant snorting from the mare before she was safely bestowed with the foal at her feet. The last Henrietta saw of her was the massive head, with its soft dark eyes, looking at her from over the back boards.

The snow was falling in earnest now and she discovered that she was stiff with cold. She must look a perfect fright, she thought crossly, eyeing Marnix, who, once more in his coat, looked exactly the same as usual. He spoke before she could look away. 'That was generous of you, Miss Brodie; you were quite entitled to walk away and leave me to it.' He stretched hugely, the snow powdering his dark head. 'May I offer you a lift back to the village?'

It would have been silly to have refused; for one thing she was finding it difficult to move, let alone walk, and she was cold. She said with a politeness to match his: 'Thank you, I should be glad of that,' and started back towards the road, looking, she hoped, coolly dignified. It was a pity that she stumbled and would have fallen but for his hand.

'Circumstances alter cases,' he pointed out, and took her arm until they had reached the Range Rover, but that was all he said. Henrietta sat beside him, longing with all her heart to say so much, to ask so many questions, but pride had her tongue and with every minute it became harder to speak. It wasn't until they had reached the village that he said: 'Would you mind if we go straight to the castle before I drop you off? I want to telephone the vet.'

It would have been churlish to have refused. She agreed in a wooden voice and resolved to stay in the car, or better still, get out of it as soon as he had gone inside, and nip back to her own little house. But this resolve was frustrated, for as he drove over the bridge the castle door was opened by Klara, to reveal Jonkvrouw van Hessel standing just inside, waiting for them. Henrietta got out reluctantly, mumbling that she would go home at once, but no one took any notice of her, she found herself in the hall and crossing it with her hostess, and in the sitting room she was sat in a chair and plied with coffee, hot and sweet and lavishly topped with cream. She sat on the edge of her chair, expecting at any minute that Marnix would come in, but he didn't, and presently when she declared that she should go home, her hostess rang for Klara, took a kindly leave of her and handed her over to the housekeeper, who in her turn, led her to the door and ushered her out. The Range Rover was still outside, but it was Jan behind the wheel and no sign of Marnix. With a fine disregard for her own words, she railed silently against him; leaving her like that without so much as a word— the least he could have done was to have thanked her!

She wished Jan good-bye at her door and went inside, still fuming. If he didn't want to see her, then he should keep out of her way, she told Henry with a fine logic, she for her part never wished to see him again—the mere thought brought tears to her eyes and she flung her damp things down anyhow in the dining room and pulled off her boots; presently she would go upstairs and change—but now she sat down dejectedly in a chair. Perhaps she should go back to England after all, then Mevrouw van der Zande could come and live in her little house and she would never need to see Mar-

nix again. As he had told her, she had only to agree
to let the lady have it...but she didn't want to; she
told Henry so in a loud angry voice, adding that
she hated Jonkheer van Hessel with all her heart,
that Loes was a wretched two-faced girl who deserved nothing better than the man for a husband,
that the village of Gijzelmortel, indeed, the whole
of Holland, was a complete washout as far as she
was concerned.

She got to her feet; she would have to change
her clothes, although there was no one to care if
she should die of pneumonia. It was the faintest of
sounds which made her pause and glance out of
the window into the snow-covered garden. The
owner of the castle was climbing the end wall; as
she stared he jumped with the agility of a much
younger man on to the patch of ground she had
been digging only the previous day. Before she
could reach the door he had opened it and come
in.

Her voice held faint hysteria. 'How dare you
climb my wall—is this your idea of a joke?'

He was taking off his sheepskin jacket. 'A
joke?' he repeated. 'My dearest Miss Brodie, it is
no joke. Loving you is no laughing matter—as I
have discovered to my cost. For these last few
weeks I have been fighting a rearguard action
against you, knowing that I was lost from the first
moment I clapped eyes upon you.' He smiled at

her tenderly. 'Kneeling there under the sink and telling me to go away; teaching me to mind my manners. And then that night in the cold and snow, standing by that ridiculous car of yours, looking like a small lost child frightened of the dark, and then when we had parted on one of our frequent quarrels, you came on the instant when we needed help with those poor souls—looking at those shocking sights without flinching and doing what had to be done so well and with such kindness.'

He started to cross the little room towards her. 'Oh, you have disturbed my quiet, well-ordered life, my darling heart, so that now I no longer wish to live quietly—indeed, if you will not have me, I no longer wish to live. You will exasperate me and bewitch me and delight me until the end of my days, and being the woman you are, you will most likely present me with a succession of small van Hessels and expect me to be a good father to them.'

He had come to stand in front of her, very close. Henrietta stood quite still and it seemed to her that the wild beating of her heart rocked her on her feet. All she could manage was 'Oh, Marnix,' in a funny little voice which didn't sound like hers at all, but it was apparently sufficient encouragement for him, for he caught her close in his arms and when she looked up at him he kissed her in the most satisfying fashion. When she had her breath again she asked into his shoulder: 'Why did you come over the wall?'

She felt his laugh. 'But, my darling, you told me that you would never open your door to me again, so it had to be the wall.'

He lifted her chin with a gentle hand and smiled down at her, his grey eyes very bright. 'Will you marry me, Henrietta? I'm middle-aged and ill-tempered at times, and I do like my own way, but I love you.'

She was sure of that, studying his face—and never mind the ill-temper, and what was forty for a man? The prime of life—besides, she had never given that a thought—not once, but there was something she wanted to know before she answered, but instead of the question she was going to ask she found herself saying: 'Oh, Marnix, I love you too.'

He wasn't a man to miss an opportunity; she was kissed without haste and even more thoroughly than previously. All the same, she managed: 'Loes?'

'My adorable Henrietta, I'll have to go back a bit to explain Loes. I fell in love, a long time ago now, so long that I can't remember what the girl looked like—it didn't last, but the blow to my pride did. I had plenty of work and a great many friends, and I promised myself then that when I married I would let my head and not my heart choose the girl—a young, malleable girl of whom I might be fond, but no more than that. You see, my darling, I turned against falling in love and marriage and I thought that I could arrange my life to suit myself. When Loes came here to live she seemed to be the perfect wife whom I had imagined—quiet and sweet and kind. How wrong I was!'

'But you must have known what she was like—you knew her well...'

He shook his head. 'I didn't. I only saw her as someone who would fit nicely into my own way of life. And then you came along and I knew in those first few seconds how wrong I had been. All the same, I pretended to myself that you didn't matter. I even spent a great deal of time with Loes so that I might forget you, and when we met, I tried deliberately to make you angry, telling myself that if I saw you in a temper, I should be able to dislike you.' He laughed a little. 'It made no difference at all; I was hopelessly in love with you by then, and you are quite enchanting when you are cross.'

'Loes went away,' persisted Henrietta.

'Because I told her that I was going to marry you or no one.'

'Well—' she leaned back in his arms to frown up at him. 'You hadn't even asked me... You were simply horrid—Miss Brodie this and Miss Brodie that, and leaving me to stand in the pouring rain and beg to have a leak mended...'

'I told you that I have a nasty temper, and you forget that I didn't know about Engelina, my darling—I thought that it was you Pieter called to see.' His eyes twinkled. 'If you remember, we had words about that. I couldn't bear the thought of you looking at another man—you see how unpleasant I am, my dearest? Though only when I don't get my own way.' He paused and kissed the top of her head. 'I love the way your hair curls round the edges—you are so very beautiful,' he sighed, 'and oh, my dear, I thought that I had lost you.'

'But you came...'

'Do you remember what you said in the field this afternoon?' and when she nodded: 'You didn't only say that you were glad to see me; your face, my love, when you caught sight of me...and you had had no time to pretend otherwise—such a small thing, but enough.'

He kissed her once more, and Henry, watching them from his tea cosy, mewed inquiringly; it was his tea-time and he was hungry. He caught Henrietta's eye and she said: 'The poor darling, he wants his tea,' then forgot him to ask: 'Why did you always call me Miss Brodie?'

'If I hadn't called you Miss Brodie I would have called you my darling, my darling.'

'Oh,' said Henrietta, and smiled at him quite radiantly. 'I must feed Henry.'

'Of course, my darling, but I see that he has settled down again for the moment. It would be a shame to disturb him and I can think of several things to do...'

'Oh, so can I, Marnix my dear!' She stretched up in her stockinged feet and put her arms round his neck and kissed him.

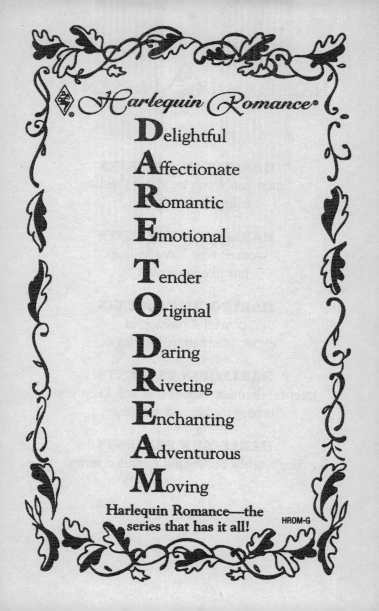

Harlequin Romance®

Delightful

Affectionate

Romantic

Emotional

Tender

Original

Daring

Riveting

Enchanting

Adventurous

Moving

Harlequin Romance—the series that has it all!

HROM-G

HARLEQUIN PRESENTS

HARLEQUIN PRESENTS
men you won't be able to resist
falling in love with...

HARLEQUIN PRESENTS
women who have feelings
just like your own...

HARLEQUIN PRESENTS
powerful passion in
exotic international settings...

HARLEQUIN PRESENTS
intense, dramatic stories that will keep you
turning to the very last page...

HARLEQUIN PRESENTS
The world's bestselling romance series!

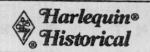

Harlequin® Historical

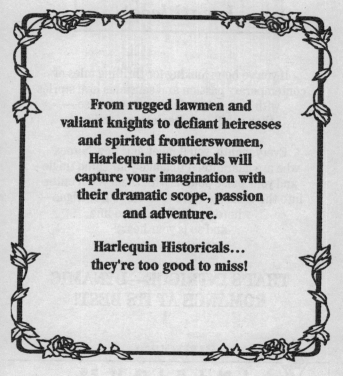

From rugged lawmen and
valiant knights to defiant heiresses
and spirited frontierswomen,
Harlequin Historicals will
capture your imagination with
their dramatic scope, passion
and adventure.

Harlequin Historicals...
they're too good to miss!